An Answering Flame

Horseback Nurse in an Adverse Land

by

C. Margo Mowbray

C. Margo Mowbray

Photo on cover:
Nurse crossing Middle Fork of the Kentucky River,
Leslie County, Kentucky
– courtesy of Frontier Nursing Service.

Photo on back cover:
Doris Reid, R.N., C.M. with twins she delivered,
Hyden, Kentucky
– courtesy of Reid family.

Copyright © 2013 C. Margo Mowbray
All rights reserved.
ISBN: 1484150287
ISBN 13: 9781484150283
Library of Congress Control Number: 2013908069
CreateSpace Independent Publishing Platform
North Charleston, South Carolina

DEDICATION:
To all Frontier nurses – past, present and future.

Contents

Introduction

The inspiration for this novel was sparked by first-hand stories of my aunt Doris Reid, who served the Frontier Nursing Service during World War II. The remarkable story of the privately-funded FNS has inspired talented and passionate writers before me. There are academic papers, biographies, photographs, an oral history project that includes one hundred and ninety-two personal interviews; founder Mary Breckinridge's autobiography, memoirs, documentary films, and children's books.

Fortunately, the FNS has always valued thorough records. Archives abound with no-nonsense accounts of its purpose, accomplishments, challenges and needs as the nurses carried out their mission in Kentucky's Appalachia.

Once you got to know Doris, she seemed a lot taller than five-foot-one-inch. She had enormous presence – something that Mrs. Breckinridge looked for in her nurses – something she called "the ability to enter a sickroom and absorb all their fears and transform them into confidence."

I relied on Doris's self-published memoir, *Saddlebags Full of Memories*, which she brought to my mother in the late 1980s in the form of a hundred hand-written yellow legal-size pages. Of her many adventures, only the most unusual and unnerving made it into her book. More than forty years had already passed since Doris's Kentucky experience. I did not want another forty years to pass without sharing her stories for wider appreciation.

Doris was no more heroic than any of the women and men who served in the FNS. Attempting an account of each remarkable situation, the many dedicated people involved, and the challenges they overcame would have required efforts too herculean for a writer.

This is a fictional work, drawing upon stories I discovered in diverse and factual sources. My hope is that in collecting the stories of many and having liberated myself from a strict chronological account, I have told a larger truth. The real people behind these stories saved lives and sacrificed their own comfort to give comfort and care to others. The FNS measurably raised life expectancy and the quality of life in the mountains of eastern Kentucky – an accomplishment as monumental to those folks as changing the spin of our planet.

All characters in this novel were inspired by actual people and events. Somewhere between the actual person and their spirit lies the character. I have used the characters to compile episodes into the realm of Doris's five-plus years with the FNS. I feel I have provided the reader an accurate account of what life was like in the FNS and its service area during that time. From our comfortable lifestyles at the beginning of the twenty-first century, it's a stretch to place ourselves in the milieu of this anachronistic frontier. The locals I came to know didn't say much about the struggles that were common to their forebears. I had to imagine washing clothes without electricity or running water; preserving a year's meat with no refrigeration; the heat of a late summer day spent canning vegetables over a wood stove; and enduring winter months with nothing green to eat but pickles.

I am proud to introduce you to these people, both within the FNS and those they served. I admire them as resourceful, self-reliant and courageous.

I hope you will enter their world wholeheartedly – these stalwart folks deserve no less.

They can inspire us all.

Frontier Nursing Service
approximate service area
Leslie, Clay and Perry Counties,
Kentucky

Prologue

"It's another Hell-for-Certain baby . . . "

— Frontier Nurse Nancy Langston

---

*N*ancy's eyes stung from the sleet as her horse lunged to cross the rocky creek again. She was on her way up Hell-for-Certain Creek in the fading light of the January afternoon, in response to the man's urgent plea for her help. Some miles up the rugged path, a family anticipated her arrival.

"I hope Nurse Nancy ain't overlong in comin'," the boy said, bursting out of the light-starved log cabin, the rickety door slapping behind him. There was nothing he, his brothers, or sisters could do to ease their mother's spells of gripping pain. Their father had ridden the mule down the creek to fetch the nurse. This time of year, Hell-for-Certain Creek was sure to live up to its name.

Inside, the two youngest children sat wrapped in a quilt on a bench in the small room. Henry, the oldest boy, had been left in charge, which was fine as long as their mother would just lay quiet and peaceful. But when she flailed and clenched the peeled posts of the hand-made bedstead, her fists turned sheet-white and it frightened the children. Her face was wet with sweat, even though it was so cold in the cabin they could see their breath if they stepped away from the open fire on the grate. The burning pine log crackled and popped, sending sparks out onto the stone hearth. A lard can nearly full of spring water hung on a rod above the fire, but it was awfully slow to boil.

The boy hugged himself to keep from shivering and peered into the dimness of the overgrown path. The sleet was turning to snow, and the ground was getting slick. In a moment he heard a horse, the puddles amplifying its footfalls. "She's here!" Emmet shouted toward the cabin, as the horse and rider emerged from the woods. The boy reached up to hold the reins while the nurse swung about and dismounted, her bright yellow slicker sending droplets about in gauzy streaks. Her face was ruddy but her nose was whitened by the chill. She stamped her leather boots a few times, removed the saddlebags that contained her delivery kit and walked purposefully to the cabin. At a time like this, she couldn't yield to her fatigue, even if her mission took many hours. She knocked while entering and disappeared into the dark room to catch another baby.

Nancy greeted the family by their first names, yanking off her wool gloves. She hung her slicker and wool cap on a peg, keeping her warm sweater on for the time being. Althea was beginning the hard stage of labor, and the nurse was grateful that the father had come for her when he did. This was the woman's sixth birth, so the baby could come very soon. Had Nancy been summoned any earlier, she would have had to close her outpost clinic early and send the waiting families and children home without the care they needed that day. But births never seem to occur at convenient times for anyone but the baby. Her colleagues always quipped that most babies arrive in the middle of the night. This one was a pleasant surprise – at least her ride up the rocky creek was mostly in daylight – what daylight managed to reach into the narrow hollow.

The nurse began by laying clean newspaper over the small table the family had placed near the woman's bed. Someone had thoughtfully brought a cane-bottom chair next to it for the nurse to sit on in case there was any waiting to be done. In the fast-fading light she reached into her large saddlebags, her hands knowing where every item was to be found and where it was to be placed.

Turning to the tall boy with dark tousled hair, she said, "Henry, can you make sure all your coal oil lamps are full and the glass is clean for us?"

"Already done, Miss Nancy," he replied. "Daddy had me to do it when Mother started her miseries."

She unpacked a series of nested basins, then checked the water in the lard can, dipped some into the largest basin and washed her hands. She tied on her crisp white apron and paused a moment. Holding her hands in front of her, she asked Hattie to come tuck her damp hair up under her nurse's cap. "I should have done this before I washed up," she said, more to herself than anyone else.

After bending down for the girl, she coerced herself to return to erect and turned away from all of them just long enough to close her eyes and take a long, deep breath.

To the children she now looked very nurse-like, except for her riding britches and mud-streaked black boots. They were too young to recognize the exhaustion in her face.

She set up a small Sterno can, lit it, and placed a shallow basin over the heat. As Nancy began sterilizing her instruments, the small children sat watching her, wide-eyed. Althea tried to muffle a gasp, so Hattie started to lead the younger ones into the back room. "You children may stay in here where it's warm," the nurse told them in a kindly voice. "Your mommy is okay. This is just like seeing a new lamb into the world. Don't be alarmed if there's some blood. It's purely natural."

The children said nothing and sat very still.

"You boys make sure we have enough wood to keep the fire going strong so it stays warm for your mother and your new baby. Hattie, can you find me another empty lard can so I can place it near the bed? We're going to need it."

Hattie, the oldest girl at fourteen, stepped away just long enough to lift the heavy cast iron burner to add a chunk of wood to the kitchen stove. She checked the kettle heating on it and silently returned with the lard can and slipped into the shadows not far from her mother's bed.

The father appeared after tending to the mule and the nurse's horse. He did his best to seal up the gaps in the wooden shutters. He then began lighting the oil lamps, placing each in a way to help the nurse see. The light from the lamps tamed the huge shadows the fire was throwing at the dark walls. Sleet pattered on the roof. Another labor pain gripped Althea, who gulped a breath and panted it out yet did not complain.

The midwife was to have a syringe of Ergotrate ready in case the mother began to hemorrhage, the most common and serious birth complication for the mother. To her horror, Nancy did not find the vial, and suddenly realized that she had not packed it. She had intended to take a fresh supply from her clinic stock and place it in her bag that afternoon, but got distracted and never returned to it. When the father came for her, she'd overlooked it.

The baby's head appeared in the ideal position, facing backwards. The nurse was very grateful for this normal presentation. It was then she realized she'd forgotten to slip on her rubber gloves; worse yet, she had neglected boiling them to sterilize them, which should have been part of her preparation when she had the time. Now it was too late. All she had time to do was lubricate her bare hands with mineral oil, and guide the baby's head and first shoulder out. She tried to soothe her rattled nerves by recalling that the old granny midwives just smeared lard on their hands to deliver a baby.

There was no time to dwell on any of that.

"Can you give another push now, Althea? The hardest part is almost over."

It was time to turn the baby gently to clear the second shoulder. The baby came smoothly and easily now.

"You've got another beautiful baby girl, Althea!"

The nurse cleared the baby's nose and mouth, and the newborn assured everyone that she was fine with her first little bellow. Nancy felt the umbilical cord between her two fingers and when the pulse faded to nothing, she clamped off the cord in two places and snipped it with her sterilized scissors, wiped the baby off, and placed her on the mother. During the brief lull between the birth of the baby and the afterbirth, the nurse scolded herself about her inexcusable oversight regarding the anti-bleeding drug.

Her thoughts returned to her current task. Silently praying for Althea, she asked the mother for "one more good push," to coax out the placenta. This was the critical time for the mother, since a torn uterus could hemorrhage and be fatal without the shot of Ergotrate. Again the rubber glove oversight disturbed Nancy deeply. If a mother hemorrhaged, the nurse, wearing a sterile glove, needed to reach into the uterus to pinch off the bleeding until the drug took effect. The only other remedy would be to prop the foot of the bed up to elevate the woman's pelvis and hope that the bleeding stopped before it was too late.

Nancy sat listlessly by the mother, holding in her tension so it would not cloud Althea's peaceful moment as the critical seconds passed. She hadn't noticed when Hattie left her station for the kitchen. The smell of biscuits and frying back bacon brought the nurse out of her silent angst. Relief began to replace her anxiety when there was no sign of trouble. Althea was recovering normally.

Mother and nurse were both exhausted, but not the newborn, who of course demanded attention. Nancy bathed her and wrapped her in the new receiving blanket she'd brought for the delivery.

It was a mountain tradition for the family to invite the nurse to share in a meal and "take the night" in these Appalachian homes, but when Nancy counted beds, it looked to be a pretty tight fit. She gladly accepted the plain but filling hot meal, and decided to ride back to her outpost clinic at Bullskin Creek. Surely, the chilly night air and adrenaline would keep her alert.

"I'll foller you back home, to see that you come to no harm, ma'am. It's untelling how bad the creek mought be by now," the father declared. Nancy did not discourage him, glad for the security of the local woodsman for the return ride down the treacherous creek. Alone, who would know if she had an accident or a displeasing encounter with a suspicious moonshiner who didn't recognize her in the dark?

She re-packed her saddlebags and dressed for her ride out. Once the father left the cabin to get the animals ready, Emmet approached the nurse. "I heer'd it mought bring good luck," he said softly, "so I put Daddy's axe under Mommy's bed today." There was an old mountain superstition that an axe placed under the bed would "cut the fever" and bring faster healing.

"I knowed it worked, cuz I was wishin' fer a sister," he added.

Nancy gave him a long, silent hug. Nurses were supposed to be strong, so she was glad he couldn't see her tears.

Settled in beneath her own quilt sometime after midnight, Nancy tried to tally the births she'd attended in the last several weeks. She was losing track of the families, the babies, and the weeks. What alarmed her most was her forgetfulness about the critical medication. She had been drilled again and again on the correct way to attend these log cabin births, regardless of the conditions. This time her attention had lapsed and she had not followed the exact technique the Frontier Nursing Service taught. Her mistakes could have cost Althea her life. The woman could have bled profusely. Her skin would have lost all color as she lapsed into shock, her revival doubtful. The nurse shuddered at the thought of that kind of outcome in front of her – now six – children and husband.

There used to be barely enough nurse-midwives to tend the ten thousand folks scattered up these hollows. But with the war on in Europe, almost half of the trained nurse-midwives had left for Britain, leaving too few to cover this seven hundred square miles of Kentucky backcountry. Nancy started to doubt her abilities as a nurse-midwife. "Things will look better after a good night's sleep," she reassured herself. "My prayer for now is that no more babies decide tonight is the time to make their break for the outside world."

Fatigue overwhelmed her last waking thought, *how much longer before there are more nurse-midwives to help us take care of these people?*

An Answering Flame

"Heaven is a Kentucky kind of place."

— attributed to a pioneer Methodist minister

"*I*magine it! Nurses on horseback," Evelyn exclaimed, shaking the newspaper she was clutching in her excitement. She began reading the advertisement aloud,

> **Attention Nurse Graduates with a sense of
> adventure! Your own horse, your own dog and a
> thousand miles of Kentucky mountains to serve.
> Living quarters and board at reasonable rates;
> six weeks paid vacation each year. Apply Frontier
> Nursing Service, Wendover, Kentucky.**

"I'm going to apply for an opening right now!" she resolutely added, handing the newspaper to Donna.

The two young women were sharing a sandwich during a precious break from their nursing duties at the hospital in Petoskey, Michigan. They had become friends in spite of their differences. Evelyn was raised in Ann Arbor, a college town downstate. Her father was a college biology professor, and her mother was a secretary for an executive in a manufacturing plant. Evelyn's pretty hands told of a privileged youth. Her parents had sent her to a fine college in Baltimore where she graduated with a nursing degree. Her shiny brown hair was always carefully gathered and made an attractive mounting for her starched white nurse cap and prestigious Johns Hopkins pin.

"All we did for fun was dress up and have dinner in my parents' friends' homes. My father is always trying to fix me up with some boring graduate student . . . some fellow with thick glasses and bitten fingernails," she complained to Donna. "My father thinks

I should be happy staying at home while my wealthy husband has his career! Sure I have my own car, but they don't let me drive it!" It was clear this lifestyle didn't suit Evelyn. She decided to leave the boredom and predictability of her hometown and family. She had spent summers at their cottage in the shorefront village of Harbor Springs, just around the shore of Lake Michigan from Petoskey, so she applied at the local hospital and got a nursing job. But it was apparent the short move to the "tip of Michigan's mitten" had not satisfied her restlessness.

Donna Carroll was born and raised on a small farm near Burt Lake, only a dozen miles south of Petoskey. Her father was a carpenter. When the cold winds and hard freezes choked out that kind of work, he rustled up handy-man jobs, doing anything people would hire him for, to provide for his family of four children. There was always a garden, fishing, and canning foods to minimize the need to go to town and spend money on groceries.

Donna's combed-back, cropped hair was the color of red willows in the late evening sun. Freckles crowded each other on her nose and hands, telling of many hours tying up tomato vines and pulling weeds between hills of corn and beans. Donna had thrown herself into nurse training just as she would have hoeing or harvesting. It wasn't easy for her, but she was determined to finish. She knew that with a nurse's qualifications, she could expect steady year-round paying work.

Once in a while the two young women would go to Donna's family's old farmhouse for an overnight. "It's so *quaint,*" Evelyn would say. She loved Aunt Myra's blackberry pancakes, and the family grew the best corn-on-the-cob she had ever eaten.

Carroll family roots ran deep in the community. There was shock and a huge sense of loss when news spread of Donna's mother's sudden death of coronary failure.

"She had such a big heart, I guess she just gave most of it to others, and didn't leave any of it for herself," one neighbor said at the funeral. The Carrolls had been a close family. Donna and her twin sister Delores adored their big brother Earl, and all of them were endeared of little Katie, who was much younger. With their mother gone, it wasn't too many years before the family ties began loosening: Earl left for a job in distant Florida; Delores married and moved out west; and because Katie was so young when their mother died, their aunt Myra took her in.

Donna had no desire to leave. She found comfort alone in her beloved northern woods, under the protective canopy of the maple forest in summer. She liked to feel the damp earth yielding silently beneath her feet after the snowmelt. Spring blossoms and the spectacular colors of the hardwood foliage in fall usually cheered her. Though she never dwelled on her talents, Donna inherited her mother's desire to give heartfelt care to others.

Sitting in the bright light of the staff break area, Donna finished reading the advertisement that had so excited Evelyn. With the war on, the Frontier Nursing Service had seen some of their key staff return to Britain, and they desperately needed replacement nurses.

Evelyn interrupted her thoughts. "With our training, they'd hire *both* of us. Oh, Donna, why don't you apply too? It'll be like summer camp, only we'd get *paid!*"

Evelyn acted on her impulse, and two weeks later her acceptance letter arrived from the Frontier Nursing Service. She quit her job and in a breathless flurry, left for Kentucky.

"A thousand miles of Kentucky mountains" repeated in Donna's mind like a church hymn chorus for the next few weeks. She kept thinking of those nurses leaving peaceful Kentucky to go to England, where German bombs were dropping on people's homes. "Why can't I be like Evelyn and just go?" she scolded herself.

Maybe it was the cold, black and white winter evening, but for some reason that night the heartache that began after the loss of her mother returned and lodged in Donna's chest. With Evelyn and her enthusiasm so far away, Donna was left with her own thoughts. Nursing in the surgery room was very demanding, but it didn't mask the emptiness. This wasn't the kind of job Donna had imagined nursing would be. Some days she felt detached from the patients who came in for surgery. She only knew them by what was written on their charts.

That winter evening, Donna finished her shift, found the advertisement she and Evelyn had clipped about the Frontier Nursing Service, and re-read it for the twentieth time. But this time a single word jumped out at her. She felt a shift deep in her chest: "*serve.*" It was the lever she needed to make the decision.

"I will apply. They need me more than I'm needed here."

A letter from the Frontier Nursing Service arrived two weeks later. As Donna handled the envelope with the insignia of the nurse on a lunging horse, her heart raced. She had been accepted, and the FNS strongly suggested she make travel plans "as soon as possible within reason." As a post script, she was to notify them of her measurements "in order to be properly fit for your uniform." Guided by the feeling that she was answering a plea to a higher cause, she found her supervisor and gave two weeks' termination notice. With a steady hand, Donna wrote back to the Frontier Nursing Service to say she would leave for Wendover, as soon as her two weeks were up. With that one simple sentence, she pledged her nursing skills to the people of southeast Kentucky, and her life changed forever.

She was exchanging her steady job in the surgical department of Petoskey's hospital for the unknown. Severing the security of having family close by "is like cutting stalks of corn in the fall," she thought. "You've got to cut them down or you can't plant a new crop."

In January of 1942, just a month after the Pearl Harbor bombing, twenty-nine-year-old Donna Carroll left the only home she'd ever known and found herself and one suitcase three states away at the train station in Hazard, Kentucky, waiting for a total stranger to pick her up.

On the train, Donna had been almost too excited to eat, but sensibly ordered a hot breakfast in the diner before her final stop. Because the war had already begun to affect passenger travel, the

diner car setting was spartan and without linens; the steward removed her coffee cup as she was being seated because they had
run out of coffee. There was no sugar for her hot cereal, but she
cared little about luxuries like that. She forced down the last bite
of oatmeal and brought her luggage alongside the vestibule window to await the next stop. The gathering light silhouetted steep,
black hill shapes that looked very close to someone from the open
rolling Great Lakes country.

The morning air was crisp. There were ice crystals on the landing. A muddy Model A Ford lurched to a stop in front of the station. She recognized the Frontier Nursing Service insignia on its
door. "Everyone knows they stopped building those back in the
twenties," Donna thought. The solo driver, a round-faced girl in
her mid-twenties with light wavy hair showing beneath her wool
cap, motioned Donna over with a day-brightening smile.

"I'm Ardice, but everyone calls me 'Dicey,' " she said, as she
popped the clutch, nearly killing the old Ford's motor. The twenty-
five mile-long ride on narrow gravel roads wound through country
that looked to Donna as if the Creator had poured out a bag of giant mismatched marbles now overgrown with trees. Ardice, accustomed to bringing new staff in from the railroad depot, proudly
announced that "the only flat part of this country is the surface of
calm water, and there isn't very much of that!" The bare trees were
laced with hoarfrost. The underbrush was dense and the hillsides
were splashed with evergreens. Creeks, jumbled with ice, cut the
steep banks randomly on both sides of the road, some barely a few
dozen yards apart.

Ardice announced they were nearly there as the headquarters
buildings at Wendover came into view above the main road. "Just
leave your luggage in the car," she said, "because your dorm room
is down in Hyden and I'll take you there after dinner."

Donna could see the Middle Fork of the Kentucky now, a dark
channel between icy banks some distance below the buildings.
The gravel crunched under their feet and bleak winter sun came
through the dormant hardwoods. Donna took a deep breath and
caught the scent of the beautiful evergreens that stippled the hills.

There was no time to think about her surroundings. Ardice escorted her into the two-story log building they called the "Garden

House," slipped behind the desk, and on a manual Underwood typewriter pecked the beginning entries of Donna's permanent file. Ardice then escorted her into the next room and introduced her to the Assistant Director, Dorothy Buck.

As a registered nurse, Miss Buck explained, Donna could expect to be assigned to the Hyden Hospital or sent out for "floater duty," meaning she'd be working the several outlying clinic locations as needed. Her allowance was ten dollars a month, with room and board provided. Miss Buck gave Donna a collection of typed instructions and a list of articles she would be responsible for. Donna was assigned her outdoor Frontier Nursing Service uniforms: English-style tan riding breeches, tall leather riding boots, a bright yellow hooded rain cape split up the back for horseback riding, the belted wool jacket for winter; a denim vest for warmer weather. "FNS" was crisply embroidered on the left shoulder of the jacket. She felt the weight of responsibility as Miss Buck handed her a pair of handsome custom-made leather saddle bags with a spotless removable fabric liner.

A young lady, one of the "couriers" in a white shirt and belted slacks, gave Donna a tour of Wendover's facilities – the dorms above the Garden House office, the small clinic and outbuildings that included a stout oak barn. She pointed out Mrs. Breckinridge's log residence and personal headquarters, which they called the "big house." Once outside, Donna heard the measured clangs of a blacksmith's rounding hammer. She could see one of the dozens of handsome FNS horses standing relaxed in front of the forge shed. The smell of red-hot iron and the quick "skitch" sound of a hot shoe dropping in a bucket of cooling water made her wonder about the horse she would be assigned. This horse was tall, maybe sixteen hands at his withers, about three inches over the top of Donna's head, not an ideal matchup. "I guess once you're on top of a horse, his height doesn't matter," thought Donna, "but I wonder if they'll let me carry a ladder!"

Big house at Wendover as it appeared in 2010. Built in 1925, it served as Mrs. Breckinridge's residence and personal headquarters — *Author photo.*

Original "Garden House" building at Wendover, used for administration and courier dormitories — *courtesy of FNS.*

It was Mrs. Breckinridge's custom that after arriving, all new hires had their first meal with her in the big house. Ardice ushered Donna into the front room of the big homey building to meet the tireless founder and Director of the Frontier Nursing Service. Mrs. Breckinridge stood up, her arms open in a warm greeting. She had short windblown gray hair but her face did not look sixty-one years old. There was a depth to her large blue eyes that suggested an unforgotten loss.

They were joined by several other staffers. After introductions they found seats in the large dining room. Donna waited until the others pulled out their straight-back cane-bottom chairs and sat down before she seated herself. The conversation during the meal was lively and intellectually challenging. Mrs. Breckinridge had a knack for finding people to serve her Frontier Nursing Service with what she called "a deeper motive than a search for adventure." With seventeen years' experience hiring and managing people suited for this unique service, Mrs. Breckinridge was skilled at directing the repartee. She concluded their conversation by looking Donna right in the eye, saying, "Heaven knows, my dear, a willingness to accept misadventure must be part of your mental equipment." In spite of the forewarning, Donna didn't show her unease. Mrs. Breckinridge, able to assess a person's character quickly, was confident that Donna would fit in perfectly, once she fully understood the mission. Taking Donna's hand in both of hers, she smiled and recited a snippet of the speech made at the dedication of the Frontier Nursing Service Hospital in 1928:

"The beacon lighted here will find an answering flame wherever human hearts are touched."

Releasing Donna's hand, her only parting thought was how they'd find this stubby new nurse a suitable horse. She could not recall any in the stable less than fifteen hands. Regardless, Mrs. Breckinridge expected everyone around her to rise to any challenge, and this was no exception. This new nurse would have to overcome any problems her sturdy but short stature might present.

As Donna left the big house on her way to Ardice's car, she spotted the horseshoer she'd seen earlier, working on a door hinge outside the oak barn. To get acquainted and to get a closer look at the horses, she stopped and introduced herself to Ellery. He wasn't tall which is an advantage when much of your labors put you in the bent-over posture of a horseshoer. He wore a leather apron over his faded dungarees. Even though the winter air was chilly, the sleeves of his blue chambray shirt were rolled up. Donna noticed his muscular forearms. He wore a felt fedora that had seen bouts of adversity, by the condition it was in.

Donna confided to him that she could pretty much face any medical situation with no fear, but her only horseback experience was with an older farm horse. "Just a grade mare about this tall to me," she said, leveling her hand at about chin height. "I still had to tie her up alongside a hay bale or a stump to get on her."

"Well," drawled Ellery, sizing up her inseam with a bashful glance, "you'll soon come to know that if Miz Breckinridge axes you to do something, you do it whether you can or not." He laid the hammer down. His hands were brawny and rough, but his voice was smooth and unhurried.

He turned toward the horses, thoughtfully looking them over and added, "There ain't none of 'em I'd call short, "but I c'n fetch you a middle-heighted one you might could do with."

Donna was comforted by his frankness. "Thank you, Ellery," she said, and held out her hand to shake. He looked at it, then hesitantly extended his after wiping it back and forth on his apron. His eyes were as blue as his shirt.

Back in the Model A for the final three miles to Hyden, Ardice headed straight for the river. Donna asked if there was a bridge. "Just a swinging bridge for walking across," Ardice replied, as she dropped into low gear and drove into the Middle Fork for the crossing. As water swirled around the floorboards, Donna asked if this was normal travel.

"Oh no . . . sometimes the river is much higher!"

They passed through the little town of Hyden and the car's gears ground before agreeing to go into low gear for the steep climb up Thousandsticks Mountain. Coming around the second switchback, Donna got her first look at the solid Kentucky sandstone hospital building and nurses' dormitory annex. Parking the car on one of the few level places in the compound, Ardice pointed out the other buildings clinging to the mountainside, including another substantial oak barn and the Mardi Cottage classroom.

Hospital at Hyden after its expansion; original
1925 sandstone portion visible at rear — *Reid
family photo.*

Hyden dormitory — *Reid family photo.*

It had been a long trip. Although parts of it had summoned her adrenaline, the journey allowed Donna the last idle moments she would enjoy for a long time.

Another courier picked up her suitcase and escorted Donna to her dormitory room. Thanking the lanky young girl, Donna pulled her door closed, set her things down, and took a moment to contemplate her new situation. She was beginning to feel some doubt about her choice to leave a steady indoor job at good pay for this frontier idea. The glitter of six weeks' paid vacation each year was fading, as she realized that it still meant forty-six weeks of duty, beating the bushes by horseback to tend sick and injured patients with nothing more than what fit in those saddlebags. She resisted the urge to kick them.

She took a deep breath to steady her uneasy mind. She recalled her past nursing experience, and some of the challenges she'd already overcome, which helped to settle her thoughts. Since she'd been assigned clinical nursing tasks beginning the very next day, there was no time to question her judgment for the moment.

Instead, she decided to go outdoors before darkness ended the day, to get a better feel for the premises. Like everyone arriving at the place, she wondered why this important facility had been situated way up on a mountain, where the road had to be carved out of the side hill. If your attention wavered, you could end up in the river a half-mile below. Donna returned to her room and finished unpacking the few things she'd brought. She sat on the bed and reflected on the events of the day and the new territory she was to call home.

Exhausted and fighting back the homesickness welling up in her heart, she decided to write home to her younger sister and Aunt Myra about her first day with the Frontier Nursing Service. Taking out pen and paper she wrote:

> *Dearest ones,*
> *As if God had jumbled His dominoes and left them all on edge, this country is more sideways than flat. The only level surface I saw today was the soup in my bowl.*
> *I haven't seen Evelyn yet, to accuse her of getting me into a real fix. I hope she hasn't slipped and fallen down in some rocky creek and can't get out. By the looks of these woods, it could happen to anyone.*
> *Ardice (Mrs. Breckinridge's personal secretary) picked me up at the Hazard train station in an old Model A. Her nickname is 'Dicey.' She said the ride to Wendover was only 25 miles, but Kentucky miles must be a lot longer than ours. They are sure more confused, as one minute you're heading one way, and the next, you've doubled back on yourself. I didn't dare admit I was getting carsick.*
> *Ardice has a nice little talk she gives, I think to scare off the faint-at-heart. She told me about poison copperheads, rattlers and the occasional rabid animal that bites someone, who the neighbors haul into the clinic for help. I assume she meant the person, not the animal!*
> *Hyden is where they are bunking me up until I get assigned to one of the outpost clinics. We will be going out on horseback to serve families who can't come to us. I knew this already, but what concerns me is that Ardice*

warned me to go slowly in getting to know the people. They tend to shoot strangers. Something about moonshine. Well, I'll stay away from that! I guess that's what they mean by Frontier Nursing Service. I half expect that our fortress will be attacked by Indians.

I had dinner with Mrs. B (Breckinridge) and several others tonight. She's a no-nonsense type, which I appreciate, but she scared me with talk of misadventure. They tell me there aren't many bears or mountain lions left, but that would be small worry compared to what I think I'm facing.

Heaven knows I am determined to make a go of my Kentucky decision. I just hope I didn't choose Hades instead. I'll write again soon.

Love as always,
Donna

She checked over her writing, then crumpled up the letter in disgust. "That's not a good letter to send anyone," she thought. So she wrote another, sealed and addressed it for posting in the morning.

Dearest ones,
I arrived safely. Ardice, Mrs. Breckinridge's personal secretary, picked me up at the Hazard train station for the nice drive to Wendover in a Ford. I'm very comfortable in my new dormitory room here in Hyden.

I knew I would be servicing patients on horseback, and they've picked out a nice short horse for me to ride on the beautiful trails. It's lovely country and I look forward to spending lots of time in the outdoors. Maybe I'll see deer. I had dinner with Mrs. B this evening. She said I'd do fine.

Love always,
Donna

Affrays, Slide Falls, Mad Dogs and the Idiot Claim

"A square dance was a wholesome way to spend an evening — as long as the hostess collected all the pistols at the door."

— from an interview with
Couriers Mardi Perry and Susan Putnam,
FNS Oral History Project, 1979

If Donna had seen the local newspapers the week she arrived in Hyden, she would have thought it a lawless place. Reports of folks shooting each other peppered the front pages. The *Thousandsticks News* reported that "two Sizemore brothers had both been shot in an affray." One was hit in the abdomen and the other was "shot slightly in the head." In a separate incident, Bradley Collins had gotten shot in the arm, and the trial of Perry County Deputy Sheriff Isaac Kilburn – accused of fatally shooting Steve Collins – was called off for "insufficient witnesses." The unspoken story might have been that no one wanted to cross the deputy in court, for fear of attracting surprise lead-based vengeance.

In fact, trials for shootings and other criminal acts were so common, people sat in the courtroom gallery for the entertainment they offered.

A tendency toward insubordination in this part of the country had deep roots you could trace to the Civil War. Kentucky had tried to remain neutral in the War between the States, but when Confederates attacked within the state in 1861, Grant's Union troops occupied Paducah. At that point, the state reluctantly declared Union loyalty. After the war, the victorious North created the Bureau of Internal Revenue to collect taxes on distilleries to help pay for Reconstruction. Resentment began to fester when revenuers – opportunists who used their Union connections to get hired for the job – made their living by tattling on their neighbors' stills.

Kentuckians have a well-deserved reputation for feistiness. In 1897 they revolted against privateers who charged for the use of their roads. A rowdy bunch destroyed toll gates and burned gate houses. They were so disruptive that the state had little choice but to abolish the practice of private tolls, and established free roads.

Not too many years after that ruckus, a political dispute erupted. The election of the governor was declared fraudulent, and in 1900 the conflict brought about Governor Goebel's assassination.

Kentucky tobacco farmers turned violent in 1904, and the "Black Patch War" began. Revolting against the monopolistic buyers, they burned warehouses and barns. They even burned the tobacco fields of the farmers who cooperated with the price-fixing big buyers. It took four years of turmoil to bring about an auction system for their tobacco crop.

The heat of old resentments may have cooled over generations, but like a grafted tree, strong characteristics became ingrained. Disdain for authority was passed down from generation to generation.

"It was never against the code of some of the mountaineers, whose land is too poor for them to eke out a living, to turn their own corn into whiskey and sell it to the neighbors," Mrs. Breckinridge explained.

Donna came from a hard-working, law-abiding family with little time for liquor and its mysterious attraction. She didn't want to appear pious, so she found an excuse to ask Ellery about a horse matter, then worked up a way to ask him about moonshining.

"I see no differ'nce between them makin' 'shine or their wife makin' jam from a razzberry patch," he told her. "Hit's their corn. Whether they eat it, drink it or sell it to somebody else, hit's their right." He stopped there. This was about the most he'd ever said on a topic. He looked at her earnestly and Donna sensed that the rest of his message might have been that any traitorous sneak who tried to gouge them for it deserves something from the business end of a Winchester.

Evelyn had heard that Donna had arrived. She was serving at Flat Creek and on her next day off, she sped to Hyden on Rusty, her tall roan gelding. After a joyous greeting, Evelyn joined the nurses for their evening meal at the dorm and recounted some of her experiences so far.

"I saw a white-cap Mennonite baptism. They go in the river – completely under water – three times! I've eaten 'boiled leather britches' which are pretty good with fried potatoes and side pork ... then there was the morning I went to pick up what I thought was a short piece of rope coiled beside the woodshed. It lifted its head and stuck its tongue out at me!" It was her first encounter with a copperhead. The others shared their own snake stories for Donna's benefit, since she was the new nurse.

Donna brought up what Ellery had said about moonshine. She knew nurses were expected to ride alone to homes in the same woods that sheltered the liquor stills.

Evelyn, in her devil-may-care way, told her not to worry.

"Once you get out in the woods, you'll be safe." Even at night, her Frontier Nursing Service uniform would protect her, Evelyn said.

"What do you mean?" Donna interjected. "How can a wool blazer and a necktie do me any good against a gunshot? As a tourniquet? We aren't supposed to use the tourniquet." She looked up at Evelyn with uneasy curiosity.

"No, dearie, the people recognize you as a nurse, and they'll let you pass. Donna, you're safer up there among the people than down in Hyden on a Saturday night!" Turning to the others, she asked, "Did you know that the windows of the courthouse were shot out again?"

"This is supposed to ease my mind?" thought Donna.

Evelyn continued without waiting for an answer. "Last week, we went to a square dance. The fiddle and guitar music was wonderful! We were popping white corn, having a lot of fun when we heard two gunshots outside. We went out to check, but all we saw were two young men disappearing into the woods. I doubt they were plinking tin cans off a fence post!"

"No wonder I don't dance," thought Donna. "I'd make an easy target the way I move." Evelyn interrupted her personal joke, adding, "We never heard anything more, so I assume there were no serious injuries."

There were no policemen in Hyden. One would not be hired until 1946. If anyone had asked, the reply might have been, "Why do we need a policeman? Our nice little village of Hyden is a town of three hundred, many of whom *are* law-abiding."

Evelyn then admitted to the others that she'd been spending some of her off-time in the Leslie County Courthouse.

"Why would you rather go there than London or Manchester?" her colleagues asked her. Their idea of fun on a precious day off was to ride the bus to a real town and see a movie, or sip a frosty chocolate soda in a cheery cafe.

"I love looking at the tidy stores all lined up on real sidewalks," one of them said.

"It's fun looking at all the pretty new things in the windows, even though I'm poor as a bird in a cage!"

"When the bus finally hits the pavement, it's like a magic carpet ride!" someone added.

But Evelyn hankered for glimpses into Kentucky's rural social life. Having come from a well-to-do family, she was agog at some of the people's situations. Then there was the official process for awarding public assistance.

"There's this thing called the 'pauper-idiot' claim," Evelyn told the group. "Unless two doctors have signed a statement for the judge, each case has to be reviewed at an open courthouse hearing. The judge and the county magistrates listen to each person's story, and decide how much money – if any – the affected person will get for care. They may be blind, or lost a leg in a coal mine or logging accident and have no means, or they could be what they call 'feeble-minded,' you know, mentally retarded. If they are unfit to manage money, a person called a 'committee' gets the allowance to care for them."

"Evelyn is right," Miss Buck said, joining their conversation. "Our Social Services department serves as committee for some eligible people in our area who don't have any kin. Sometimes unscrupulous people prey on these unfortunate people, and become their 'committee' to control the money, with little oversight."

Miss Buck continued. "The crude term 'idiot' is sometimes replaced with something just as terrible, 'feeble-minded.' Of course, now the preferred term is 'mentally-deficient' but the county still calls it the 'pauper-idiot' claim."

There was a pause as Evelyn formed her next question. "Miss Buck, do you think some of the people making these claims are children of marriages between too-close relatives – what our textbooks call 'consanguineous marriage?' " Evelyn rarely held back a question, no matter how sensitive. The other nurses squirmed awkwardly, but were secretly glad she had asked.

"That is possible, Evelyn. In highly isolated regions, you do find more occurrences of first cousins marrying. As you know, that increases the risk of the offspring to inherit recessive genes that lead to mental deficiency. You've also heard of 'double cousins' – that's when a pair of brothers have married a pair of sisters, and the children of these couples then share all four grandparents."

"One of my patients told me his cousin was also his brother-in-law. Maybe now I can figure that out," one nurse chimed in.

"It's easier to just say 'I'm kin to myself'!" another added. Some giggled at the comment but were interrupted.

"Keep in mind," Miss Buck continued, "Charles Darwin's parents were first cousins, and he in turn, married his own first cousin. Three of their sons became highly successful scientists, brilliant like their father. But the Darwins lost three children at a young age, too."

If Donna wondered whether or not there was enough work for the nurses who had accepted Mrs. Breckinridge's promise of "adventure, your own horse, your own dog and a thousand miles of Kentucky mountains," all she needed to do was read the *Hazard Herald* that same week. Alongside the advertisements for cigarettes and cough syrups were bold headlines about home accidents. Young Josephine Day of Hyden "was painfully burned on the leg while removing a pan of flaming grease from the oven." Five-year old Julia Tyree of Dry Fork died after drinking lye, and eighteen-year old Lawrence Banks was seriously injured in a slate-fall at the coal mine, and "his chance of recovery is doubtful," the story said. A ten-year-old boy had his fingers blown off while playing with a blasting cap, and yet another child needed the series of fourteen rabies shots after getting bitten, "as a result of an epidemic of mad dogs" in neighboring Perry County.

Turning the page, in between ads for "Pazo for Piles" and "Resonal for Minor Burns" there were obituaries that described lives cut short by diphtheria, tuberculosis, and the black lung.

These folks needed help well beyond the promises of drugstore patent medicines, Donna realized. Clearly there was plenty of work to keep a platoon of nurses overbusy.

"The health of the community hinges on the health of the child," Mrs. Breckinridge often said. "We bring care and education to our communities by way of each family, thus elevating its entire health and prosperity." To accomplish this, she founded the Frontier Nursing Service on three areas of emphasis: nurse-midwifery, family medicine and public health.

There wasn't much a dozen nurses could do about lingering family feuds that sometimes landed someone on an improvised stretcher bound for the hospital. But something could be done about children drinking household poisons or becoming infected with diseases like typhoid and diphtheria. The rest of the nation had pretty well conquered those preventable diseases. It was high time that Appalachia Kentucky caught up.

This spate of tragedies played out under the dark mood of the war in Europe and now, the Pacific. There was a labor vacuum left by the young men who were enlisting in the military, leaving the rugged chores of frontier survival to their women, children and older men.

Although one out of thirteen Kentucky men was overseas in the military, that still left a dozen men at home, and women were still having plenty of babies.

Decided-Against Country

"If it can be done here, it can be done anywhere."

— Mary Breckinridge

Mrs. Breckinridge made sure to spend a little time with her new hires before sending them out as another "answering flame." She had arrived in the Appalachian highlands with only the seeds of a grand plan, and within these seventeen years it had come to fruition. But it needed many more undaunted, nurturing hands in order to prove her notion that if it can be done here, it can be done anywhere.

Donna was asked to attend afternoon tea in the big house. Mrs. Breckinridge began the conversation with her conviction that "inaccessibility is a precious asset," which puzzled the young nurse. Donna always thought of assets as positive things – a full pantry, good neighbors close by, a good highway to town.

"We are proving that quality healthcare can and should be delivered anywhere in the world," Mrs. Breckinridge continued to emphasize the point. Whether or not Donna yet understood the notion, she had picked up quickly that Mrs. Breckinridge expected her to carry out the job without wavering; day or night, summer or winter.

Mrs. Breckinridge eagerly shared stories of the history of the area and her rationale in locating the Frontier Nursing Service in these mountains. She was fond of explaining that, "just one hundred and fifty years after Daniel Boone led a fearful but determined queue of white Virginia settlers through the Cumberland Gap into Kentucky, I established the Frontier Nursing Service. I chose a place they decided against – this patch of woods along the Middle Fork of the Kentucky River in remote Leslie County."

Pausing for effect, she told the nurse, "It was here in 1925, that I began building the headquarters of our Frontier Nursing Service and named it Wendover."

Why would a cultured, widowed woman select a site that the Boone party had dodged – this on-edge, sideways country laced with racing water and scrappy forest? Why forsake mother nature's swell bosom to settle on the ribs of the land, where if your mule so much as sneezed, you ran the risk of landing in the creek forty feet below?

Mary's grandfather was U. S. Vice President for James Buchanan. Her father was ambassador to Russia. Growing up, Mary lived a cultured, aristocratic life. Although she'd traveled and lived abroad, she was always drawn to the Kentucky mountains. Her wealthy grandmother was a native Kentuckian who spent much of her fortune educating Kentucky children. Mary would sit at her grandmother's knees listening to her read letters from the students she supported. Young Mary was moved by the woman's charity work. And the spirit of the mountain people went straight to her heart, germinating into a force that would direct Mary's entire life.

As a southern debutante, Mary was properly courted, found mutual love, and married an attorney. But her life took a tragic turn. Within the year her husband died of acute appendicitis. She resisted her parents' urgings to return to the security and comfort of their home. "I want to *give* service, not receive it," Mary told them. She entered nursing school, finishing in three years. Afterwards, she married a college professor and they had two children. But destiny denied her the fulfillment of raising both her cherished boy and girl; Polly was born prematurely and died within hours. Clifton "Breckie" Thompson suffered an abdominal infection and died just days after his fourth birthday. Overstrained by the double loss, Mary's marriage ended in divorce, pivoting her forever away from any traditional path.

To put her grief behind her, she took back her maiden name, and began exploring the service work that had motivated her to enter nursing school. She began by pledging to "help as many children as the number of days my dear Breckie lived." World War I had just ended, and she answered the call to serve with the American Committee for Devastated France, to help starving and homeless war orphans. It was then she became aware of the British nurse-midwives. Trained nurses added the profession of delivering babies. This practice was unheard-of in rural America, where a granny midwife showed up after a woman's labor had begun, and with hog grease on her hands, would "cotch" the baby. If the newborn didn't begin breathing right away, the granny might dip it in cold water or dose it with camphor to shock the baby back to life. She would leave for good with a dollar or two in her soiled apron pocket.

When Mary returned from overseas she was ready to settle in one place, where she could feel at home. Her mother had died, leaving her feeling unattached to much of her past. With her grandmother's inborn spirit guiding her, Mary chose Kentucky. "Such is the unity of all Kentuckians," she reflected. She had been so moved by the success of the British approach to pregnancy, birth and post-partum care that she became passionate about bringing that model to the backwoods of Kentucky.

In grade school, Mary had learned that her ancestors were warned by Cherokee Chief Dragging Canoe that settling in Kentucky, they'd find a "dark and bloody land." Although Indian attacks were a thing of the past by the twentieth century, Mary Breckinridge would face other killers in the form of botched births, epidemics of typhoid, tuberculosis and diphtheria, food poisoning, gunshots, and ailments through poor sanitation, superstitions and archaic practices that were meant to heal. The steep, isolated country posed physical barriers, but the toughest barriers would be the suspicious mountain people with their upside-down notions about how to treat sickness. Some of them were snake believers, and thought medicine was the work of the devil. If that weren't daunting enough, there were no motor roads within sixty miles, no telephones, no electricity, and no state-licensed doctor to serve a four-county region of ten thousand souls. To all of this, Mary declared, *"Where else but right here?"*

Her mother, had she lived, would have received the news as if she'd been told Mary was kidnapped by a band of marauders. This was not the future she would have envisioned for her eldest daughter. To the aristocratic matron, stereotypical Kentucky women married tobacco-spitting truck patch peddlers or moonshiners who got shot and left the poor women with a passel of children.

Mary continued making her plans, leaving the tradition of the beautiful Southern society belle to her younger sister. She brought her training and energy to the misty hollows of Leslie County where folks were still drinking out of the Middle Fork and washing their clothes with lard and lye in basins made of hollowed-out logs. According to a reliable survey, at the time Mary arrived, Leslie Countians were earning thirteen per cent of the national average income, had families twice the size of the national average, and lost more mothers in childbirth than anywhere else in the nation. These families were in desperate need of trained medical care.

"It was Dark Ages medicine," she would say, recalling the beginning years. "I knew of unlicensed men calling themselves 'doctor.' Some were truly illiterate, but I felt they were the *least* harmful because they used old folk herbs rather than more dangerous store-bought drugs. The average woman gave birth to nine children, and less than one fourth of the grannies could read and write!" Mrs. Breckinridge would take on Appalachia's eighteenth-century culture and revolutionize it. She was determined to demonstrate that quality health care could be spread successfully about this decided-against country. *"If it can be done here, it can be done anywhere,"* she repeated often.

At first, Mrs. Breckinridge was the only one who believed this could be accomplished. Coming in from beyond their mountains, she knew folks would be skeptical of her 'brought-on" ways. But Kentucky endured opposites: Union and rebel; wealth and poverty; "wet" counties and "drys" – those that had voted to outlaw beverage alcohol; the leisure of the Bluegrass elite and the labor of the coal miners. Remarkably, the two most important philosophical and political opposites of the Civil War were native Kentuckians. President Abraham Lincoln and Jefferson Davis, president of the rebel Confederate States of America, were born on Kentucky soil barely one hundred miles from one another.

These circumstances didn't daunt this motivated woman.

"I was raised among philosophical opposites. In the Civil War, two Breckinridge brothers became high-ranking officers – one in the Union Army, the other in the Confederate. In the Breckinridge home, everyone's experience was respected and their point of view heard, even if mis-matched," she explained. It was around the family dinner table that she learned the valuable skills of diplomacy and cooperation – skills she would rely upon for the rest of her life.

In the midst of poverty, moonshine and reclusive mountaineers, she bought more than three hundred acres on a south-facing hillside above a peaceful stretch of the Middle Fork of the Kentucky River. Local builders began erecting the enormous log structure that everyone soon called the big house. They chose a site where they could use the sturdiest beech tree for a lead pole to winch up the second-story logs and ridgepole. It became Mary's residence and headquarters from which she would direct the Frontier Nursing Service. To begin serving the people immediately, she stocked medical supplies and it became a temporary clinic.

Mrs. Breckinridge contracted with the federal government to become the post office, so a mail slot and sorting area was included on the main floor. Her intent was clear: "What better way to meet all our neighbors and gain their trust?"

Even before moving into the log building, Mrs. Breckinridge had drawn up plans for a twelve-bed hospital in the Leslie County seat of Hyden, three miles downriver from her headquarters. This ambitious project would multiply the efforts it had taken to build the big house at Wendover. Her strategy began with the local people, and would soon sweep in every resource she could imagine. She sat up nights making lists of prospective donors in the prosperous east coast cities. Mrs. Breckinridge packed her classic wool serge suit and string of pearls for fund-raising missions. There was a spur off the Louisville-Nashville railroad that came as far as Krypton. Mrs. Breckinridge would ride her horse to the station, fording the river seven times. Over the next few years her fundraising journeys would take her to Louisville, Cincinnati, New York, Washington, D.C., Philadelphia and any place she could curry one of her wealthy family connections. She would return to Wendover from these fundraising forays with a pledge and renewed determination to keep the projects on schedule.

By the end of 1926, her masonry crews had quarried two thousand, five hundred tawny-colored Kentucky sandstone blocks for the construction of the sturdy hospital building. The men were paid forty cents an hour.

Hence Stidham, her chief stonemason, approached Mrs. Breckinridge. "Ma'am, we were jawin' over dinner," he said, "and we made the choice to donate a day apiece on this job."

She was thrilled to have gained the support of her masonry crew, and told him so.

"We'd like to be more clever, but it would leave less to take home fer the young'uns," he said.

She had her reasons for locating the hospital up the narrow winding road on Thousandsticks Mountain. In the back of her mind were the disruptive weekend rowdies who commonly shot their guns off in town for sport.

"It's a troublesome job, and we've had no end of strife," her foreman said, resigned to the task. "Leastways it's above the ructions of Hyden on a Sat'iddy night. Hit wouldn't do to have folks in the hospital gittin' shot all over ag'in!"

While preparing her peaceful site overlooking the town, the construction crew had to overcome staggering problems. The blueprints had been donated by a Lexington architect who had never set foot on the property. The view out his office window was low, rolling hills and he had no idea that this building was to be anchored on a bench carved out of a mountain. Landslides wiped out weeks of work. The water supply was not dependable, even though the area received nearly as much rainfall as Juneau, Alaska. After four wells had been drilled and didn't prove out, Mrs. Breckinridge asked a local dowser to bring his peach tree sticks and locate water once and for all, if he had to crisscross the entire thirty-five-acre tract to find it. When a truck backed over the sloughing edge of the road and nearly tumbled to the bottom, Mrs. Breckinridge persevered.

As soon as the plumbing was working, and the Kohler gasoline-powered generators revved up to light the facility, a series of doctors began seeing patients. "It is impossible for me to reach every hoot-owl hollow in time to be of any use to a woman in childbirth," one doctor exclaimed after an exhausting ride from Owsley County.

But Mrs. Breckinridge already had a plan to solve that problem. The idea had come to her while drinking her customary four a.m. cup of black coffee: *"Decentralize."* Nursing centers would be built in a half-dozen outlying areas to bring services closer to the people. The centers would be outfitted as temporary hospitals for emergency care, so patients could be stabilized before being sent to Hyden. The buildings would be part residence and part clinic for walk-in patients. Nurse-midwives would live and work there. From each center, nurses would serve an area about a one-day horseback ride in any direction. To treat people, they would carry everything they needed inside a pair of saddlebags.

Palm and Fingers of the Helping Hand

"Work through, not for the people."

— Mary Breckinridge

The nurses cherished the times when they could break from nursing duty and join Mrs. Breckinridge in the big house for the leisurely afternoon tea or the traditional five o'clock glass of sherry and six o'clock meal. Mrs. Breckinridge would tell them of her most recent fundraising outing, or success in bargaining for a wholesale purchase, but most interesting to Donna were her stories about the local families and how the nursing centers came to be.

Mrs. Breckinridge knew that the working conditions were very difficult for her new nurses coming from civilized environments. Nurses were not accustomed to treating people in windowless cabins by the feeble glow of smoky kerosene lamps. In warm weather, snakes were common pests. Children were taught to carry a garden hoe with them to the outhouse in case of an encounter with one. In the summer there would be flies by the gross. Winters brought harsh weather and all the horseback nurse would have for protection would be a hooded slicker like those used by the Canadian Mounties. None of the nurses would have experienced travel on a horse fitted with ice nails to keep its iron shoes from slipping in the frozen creek beds. They would have to dismount frequently and with a hoof pick, chip the accumulation of ice from their horses' hooves.

To soften these hardships, Mrs. Breckinridge pictured the nursing centers as homey and appealing. "Each outpost center was to be built to appear solid and enduring, to give our families a sense of security," she said. In order to build them, she would need lots of help and resources. There was no money to hire construction crews.

Mrs. Breckinridge was vocal and persistent in her passion for bringing nursing care to the people. A quiet power grew out of her wisdom in motivating the people. It was important "to work *through* the people, not *for* them," she explained. She could not expect them to obey orders from a "fotched on" woman who wore pants and used foreign words like "patois." These were proud individuals who had gotten along by their own resourcefulness. Mrs. Breckinridge understood that she would have to earn their respect. Each of them needed to be listened out. If one person spurned her plan, it would spoil everyone against her. "It only takes one dollop of sour milk to spoil a whole pail," she said.

First she arranged a community meeting. Whole families were invited and fresh pressed cider or hot chocolate were served. "What needs to be done in order that your children can begin receiving care closer to your homes?" she would ask them.

When someone suggested that a local clinic might be built, Mrs. Breckinridge would enthusiastically agree, then suggest they begin by naming a committee. Its purpose would be to organize workings. She knew people would support the project and take pride in it if she challenged them with that responsibility. Cash was always scarce, so the committee would motivate locals to donate labor, logs, lumber and other construction items for the clinic and outbuildings. Once a committee was formed, Mrs. Breckinridge would go beyond the mountains to solicit another of her wealthy friends. With a clinic location in mind, she would suggest they donate enough money to buy the land. The only thing she could offer in return was to name the facility after them. Rarely did anyone deny her earnest appeal.

The first outpost site was sixteen miles from Hyden at Beech Fork, and named the Jessie Preston Draper Center, to honor the land donor. Building materials were shipped to Pineville, thirty-two miles away, and the only way to bring supplies in was by mule team. The round trip took four days. Mrs. Breckinridge had anticipated high flood waters and runoff from the logged-out forests above, and insisted the buildings not be placed on the lower, level ground.

At the first working, one of her committee men said, "I don't mean to give no cheek, Miz Breckinridge, but puttin' it down here on the flat would be sooner to finish hit." Mrs. Breckinridge held firmly to her plan. "They must be above the threat of the highest floods and their foundation pinnings must go deep enough to reach solid rock," she told him.

The man turned to his crew. "I swear that woman is a hunnerd pounds o' nuthin' but staunchness and pepper," he griped, but he did as he was told.

Mrs. Breckinridge then delegated construction supervision to two of her nurse-midwives, Gladys Peacock and Mary Willeford. They protested that they knew nothing of building. "Neither did I when I built Wendover, and if I can learn by doing, you can, too," she replied, and left it entirely to them. Over the next five years, variations of that process were repeated at five other locations. Clara Ford of the Henry Ford family donated the land for the Red Bird nursing center. The Ford family donated a generator for electricity and the logs from which it was built.

Red Bird Nursing Center, 2010; now a private residence — *Author photo.*

By 1929 there were six centers fanning out in the remote areas, each serving about two hundred and fifty families. Mrs. Breckinridge was fond of explaining her concept to the new nurses. "Imagine a hand with the hospital at Hyden as the palm and the outpost nursing centers as fingers, reaching benevolently into the hollows to bring health care closer to the families," she would say. The service area spread over seven hundred square miles where ten thousand people lived in the crinkled landscape, with only a dozen or so miles of actual road.

Geographically, if you started at Hyden at the three o'clock position, you could draw a rough circle clockwise to locate each facility. At four o'clock, just three miles up the Middle Fork is Wendover;

Beech Fork at five o'clock; Flat Creek, to the west on Red Bird River at eight o'clock; Red Bird at nine o'clock; Brutus at eleven o'clock; Bowlingtown at twelve o'clock; Confluence at one o'clock; then twelve miles up the Middle Fork to your starting point. The only way to travel this circuit was to trudge up and down the mountains and drainages which took a week by mule or horseback.

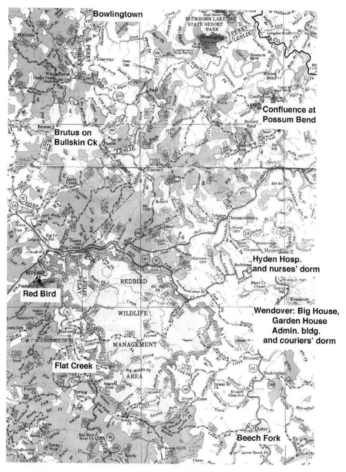

Frontier Nursing Service facilities in southeast Kentucky. *Superimposed on U. S. Forest Service map.*
Approximate locations of Wendover headquarters, Hyden hospital and six outpost nursing centers — "Palm and Fingers of the Helping Hand."

The centers, whitewashed or log, became a source of local pride. Situated handsomely above the creek bottoms, they each had a good-sized barn, chicken coop and garden spot. Locust posts fenced the perimeter with an ingenious pull-gate allowing a rider to open and close it without dismounting their horse. A levered rod lifted the drop-latch and opened the gate. It was sprung so it returned to the latched position with a second tug on the rod. Some centers had the luxury of a bathtub. There were spare bedrooms for couriers or visitors. The living areas each had a fireplace of local stone and colorful braided rag rugs to soften the hardwood floors. In the dining areas, nurses sat at handmade black walnut tables while updating detailed records of their registered families. A local girl was hired to do the household chores. She would butcher chickens, cook and clean, heat water, remove soot from the coal-burning cook stove, keep lamp chimneys clean, bring in firewood, grit corn, and can fruit and vegetables in season. The two staff nurses lived very comfortably, in spite of the demands of the job.

Mrs. Breckinridge added a cadre of volunteers, usually high school or college girls with horsemanship experience, to serve as couriers. They typically served in six-week or longer commitments, and stayed in Wendover's Garden House top-floor dorms. Boy couriers were housed in dorm rooms in the barn. Couriers made weekly rounds to the outpost centers to collect the family health records that the nurses produced. They ferried horses back and forth, escorted guests from the railroad, and did anything else they could to assist the nurses and staff. They were usually from wealthy families beyond the mountains. Exposing them to the excitement and financial realities of the operation was part of Mrs. Breckinridge's long-term strategy of sustaining financial support. The young people returned to their families brimming with stories. Their exciting adventures were featured in the FNS *Quarterly Bulletin*, which was mailed to patrons and supporters, and routinely listed current financial needs. Under "Urgent Needs" readers would see a list like:

New Horse (Including transportation from
Lexington) $190.00

8 New Nurses' Uniforms @ $3.00

2 Stethoscopes @ $2.50

Repairs to X-Ray Machine $25.50

3 10-gal. Stone Jars for Preserving Eggs $6.75

10-gal. Iron Kettle for Boiling Clothes (second-hand) $5.00

1 Bolt Terry Cloth for Kitchen Towels $6.86

New Wheelbarrow $8.35

800 ft. White Walnut (rough lumber) for Making Furniture $65.00

12 Gallons Paint for Hospital, (Put on by nurses) $35.40

Mrs. Breckinridge understood the wisdom of charging a modest fee for FNS services. She knew folks would place more value on the service that way. More importantly, charging allowed the families to retain their self-respect. Even the poorest families regarded charity with disdain. Recognizing economic realities, the FNS accepted payments over time and bartering was common.

The annual charge for a family to register with the FNS started at one dollar a year. The FNS charged five dollars to deliver a baby which included a layette – starter linens for the baby. Families could pay with fresh milk, honey, eggs, firewood, guinea hens, handmade chairs, quilts, garden produce, a couple of days' labor repairing fences or whitewashing, or whatever they could muster.

"Accept any kind of payment the family offers," Mrs. Breckinridge told the nurses. "There isn't one thing in our whole service area that isn't useful." She didn't balk when a payment came in the form of cow manure for the gardens, although the FNS was overflowing with it already, and woefully short of other supplies. "We'll use it for trading stock," she said, not wanting to hurt the man's pride as he dumped it out of his cart.

By 1929 the need for a steady doctor and medical director became critical, so Mrs. Breckinridge began searching for someone suitable. This individual would have to keep up with developments in medicine, and be hardy enough to respond to the outlying districts for patients who couldn't risk the journey to the hospital. Mrs. Breckinridge made many inquiries. She was turned down repeatedly. Her excellent relationship with Kentucky's health commissioner paid dividends. He recommended Dr. Herbert Capps of Tennessee, whose credentials were sterling. He was also highly regarded for his obstetrical record. She went to Tennessee to try to recruit him.

After an amiable luncheon, Mrs. Breckinridge got down to business. She set her cup down and looked directly into the man's eyes.

"Doctor Capps, the Frontier Nursing Service needs a doctor to serve as our medical director, who's willing to endure rural situations that one would not see in a more conventional setting." Mrs. Breckinridge struggled to find the right words. She wanted to be forthright without scaring the man off. She desperately needed someone with his abilities.

"This individual must also have a certain sense of . . . what shall I call it . . . *romance* about the atmosphere in which we function. This special person needs to stay apace with twentieth-century medical practices, yet be intrepid about responding to emergency calls in poor nineteenth century homes. There will be cases that our outpost nurses cannot handle."

The man sat quietly. He looked at his pocket watch.

"In other words, Mary, you need a full-time doctor who would also just *love* to make emergency calls on horseback up moonshine country for little or no pay."

Mary sighed. Another turndown. She was sorry that this likable man was not inclined to take the job. He would have been ideal.

"No, Doctor, I can't find any better words. That is precisely what we need. Thank you for taking time with me. Good day." She stood, as did the doctor, as a simple courtesy. Before she had a chance to turn away, he said,

"Mary, I love horses. I'll be there in two weeks."

Bootlegging, Salary Cuts and Sour Milk

"How else were we to treat these people? The ends justified the means."

— Agnes Lewis, Administrative assistant to Mrs. Breckinridge

"*I* would not have wanted my mother to know that my career included bootlegging," Mary confided to the few nurses gathered in front of the fireplace in the big house. Donna was on a brief break from her duties and was enjoying tea with the others. She leaned forward to hear every word of this part of FNS history.

Mrs. Breckinridge explained that her mother had hoped her eldest daughter would settle close by in Bluegrass Kentucky, where generations of world-famous pedigreed racing and breeding thoroughbreds are raised . . . near Lexington or Louisville, on an estate where she could stroll along the painted rail fence wearing white gloves and not get them dirty. A place to spend leisurely afternoons sipping frosty mint juleps on a shady veranda engaged in spirited repartee with titled family friends. But Donna and the nurses knew that wasn't the life for the staunch woman sitting in front of them.

All that Bluegrass refinement was a world away when Mary would jam her wool cap over her cropped gray hair and mount her trail-savvy horse at the Hazard train depot. The Kentucky that Mary chose for her home was a place in desperate need, a place that would accept her and absorb her energy and vision. This was Appalachia, where clean spring water, buckskin gloves and a sharp axe were valued over fancy cocktails, silver tea sets and damask draperies.

It was Prohibition, the thirteen-year span of time when the production, transportation and sale of alcohol had been made illegal by the Eighteenth Amendment to the U.S. Constitution. Temperance folks had pushed the ban through in hopes it would solve all the problems caused by the "devil drink." But the law did nothing to lessen the nation's craving for liquor, and enterprising scofflaws ferreted out sources of the coveted product all over moonshine country. They hired shadowy minions willing to carry the product to the cities to quench the black market for Kentucky corn whiskey. Originally strapping curved flasks inside their boots to foil the law, these runners became known as "bootleggers." As the operations got too big for the product to be hidden on the body, they came up with more brazen ways to transport it. Some law officers were susceptible to corruption and took payoffs to look the other way while runners passed through their counties loaded with "white dog."

"In this confounded country, a lot can happen that we cain't see," one marshal proclaimed. "Fer all I know, the men are a'goin' on shift at the mine." No one dared to challenge the comment, even though the stock market crash had closed the mine.

Respect for the law crumbled. A nation that voted to ban the stuff secretly demanded that it be made available to them. People lost no time exploiting the profitable side of the dilemma. One bold moonshiner set up his operation in the Bowlingtown nursing center's abandoned pump house. His rationale was sound: Who would suspect a whiskey still on FNS property?

One of the FNS horses, Lady Jean, a gray mare everyone loved, had been owned by a local moonshiner. There was a bullet forever lodged in her dappled hip.

There were no antibiotics yet. Alcohol was the only known treatment for diseases like pneumonia and other infections like trachoma. Hospitals routinely stocked straight alcohol, whiskey and brandy in their dispensaries.

"We could legally obtain alcohol, but keeping up with the permits was much more bothersome than with the narcotics," Mrs. Breckinridge explained to Donna and other nurses as they refilled their teacups.

"But the biggest obstacle was transporting it from the depot at Hazard. The officials granting us our permits had no idea what our circumstances were. We pleaded with them to allow our distributor to crate the alcohol in with our cod liver oil and other supplies, but the government would only allow it to be shipped separately and plainly labeled. Of course, Hazard was swarming with bootleggers."

Moonshine stills perched hidden among local hollows. They weren't all quart-jar operations. Some were larger producers that supplied the ravenous black market. There were obligations. Once you got caught in the vicious business, you had to produce if you valued your life. The bootleggers jealously protected their corner of the business, and they were not bashful about pulling the trigger if a stranger suddenly appeared.

"Why, Miz Breckinridge," Jonah Begley, her handyman said. "I'd be willin' to haul in your shipment o' the stuff off'n the railroad."

"I know you are willing Jonah, and I know you'd be willing to shoot it out with them too, but you'd make an easier target than I," Mrs. Breckinridge said, ending the discussion.

Not willing to put anyone else at risk, she saw no alternative but to make the trips herself. She had decided that her appearance would not arouse suspicion and her association with the FNS would provide her some protection, especially the farther away she got from Hazard. By then, the FNS was recognized and had friends among the families living along the way.

Mrs. Breckinridge had each shipment sent to a confidante in Lexington, where it was stored in an attic until she could personally retrieve it. She then packed it discreetly in her luggage and boarded the train to Hazard. She told no one that she was hauling it. Once the train let her off in Hazard, a stable boy would bring her horse to the train platform for the ride to the hospital at Hyden.

"All right, Teddy Bear, let's do our best to bring another load of medicine home again safely," she would say to her horse as they leaned into a steep part of the rutted trail. Mrs. Breckinridge shepherded many shipments of high-grade alcohol back to the hospital.

She would ride alone the two dozen miles from Hazard, through territory where cargo like hers was as good as gold.

The pints of brandy and whiskey were easy to conceal, but the gallon of straight alcohol was more challenging to pack on her horse without being noticed. The alcohol's tell-tale glub, glub, glub was even more conspicuous when ears were tuned to the outlawed substance. Until she reached more friendly territory nearer Hyden, she was terrified every time she heard someone ride up behind her. A folded paper permit from the U. S. Government was little protection from a bootlegger who was desperate to fill an order from his big city boss.

No one back home in genteel bluegrass Kentucky ever heard about the five years Mary hauled alcohol through the woods alone.

The only robbery in the history of the FNS happened during Prohibition, when a Missouri bootlegger stole one of their horses one night to make a frenzied liquor run out of the mountains. Eventually, the stolen animal was retrieved, but she was nearly ruined from hauling a heavy load many miles over rugged territory.

"She was so spent, there was the choice to leave out the poor mare from her miseries," Ellery told Donna, "but I couldn't abide, knowin' what a nervy horse she was. I took her on and brang her back up to fit." Raising clenched fists, he added, "I'd like to whup the rogue that pinched her."

Those were desperate times.

The market crash of 1929 struck a devastating blow to Mrs. Breckinridge's fundraising success. The financial catastrophe surged through her organization, necessitating a cut in all salaries and greater scrutiny in all purchasing. When cash dried up, paychecks had to be withheld until funding could be restored. Nature brought further calamity in 1930 with a winter devoid of normal rains and snow. The ground had no reserve of moisture when the scorching hot summer followed, spreading drought. In Southeast Kentucky, it parched the land and shriveled any hope of a harvest. The staff had to accept that hardship was part of life and luxury certainly was not.

Donna heard several families mention the drought, too. She asked Ellery about it when she saw him.

"Ellery, I can't imagine drought when there is so much water in this country. We have to ford creeks way up the hollows. It must have really beaten the people down."

Ellery thought a moment. "I'd not call it beaten," he replied. "People's gotta keep right on tryin' to win the battle ag'inst a life that's ever'day tryin' to rout 'em."

The FNS outposts were completed, wholly spared of any luxuries. The clinics' living facilities were functional and homey, but had no conveniences other than a deep well and a spigot-pump over the kitchen sink. Cooking was done on coal stoves and there was no electricity. In 1940 – the year General Electric produced its millionth monitor-top refrigerator for American kitchens – there still were no refrigerators in the outpost centers to keep the nurses' food from spoiling, their milk from souring, or their butter from melting.

The Wendover compound had a cave-like enclosure where food was stored to slow its spoiling in the summer heat. Mrs. Breckinridge experienced her first kerosene refrigerator when one was donated by a patron. It was a mystery to her how lighting a small fire could produce ice, but she didn't question the invention. Instead, she put her mind to thinking of some way to bring the luxury to her hard-working nurses in the six outpost centers.

"Only those who have lived and worked through hot summers without ice can understand the comfort that ice brings," Mrs. Breckinridge said to Donna one evening at Wendover as she reflected on the earlier years. She announced her desire in the *Quarterly Bulletin*, writing, "The overabundance of ice in January does nothing to refresh our nurses with iced tea or lemonade during the summer months." A wealthy patron learned of her plea while touring the centers during a blazing hot week in 1941. The woman was so impressed, she returned to her upscale home near Detroit, and mounted her own fundraising effort, calling it the "Refrigerator Fund." She spent two weeks drinking tea with her wealthy neighbors, explaining the situation. Before the summer was over, six non-electric, lamp-lit refrigerators arrived in Hyden, one for each nursing center.

Mrs. Breckinridge was overjoyed. Daily her staff endured hardships. Now she could reward them in a way that meant more than money. In a thank you letter to Mrs. Henry B. Joy for the six refrigerators, she wrote:

> *There is a wish that lives in the heart of every true nurse to give her service to those who need it most . . . a willingness to endure hardship brings nurses of a fine caliber to us. In the world beyond these mountains, they could get double and treble the salaries we are able to pay. Thus all of our staff are volunteers in part through the measure of their financial sacrifice. Your grand contribution is a way to reward them for their intrepidness.*

The woman's benevolence helped bring the centers into the twentieth century, but the perennial financial challenges were as unmoving as the stoic old beech trees at Wendover.

Gunpowder and Whiskey, and an Axe Under the Bed

"Women are fighting their own battle
right inside their homes on Kentucky soil.
Small wonder we have lost more women in childbirth in America
than men in war."

—Mary Breckinridge

The "small wonder" Mrs. Breckinridge referred to was a huge concern to her. In fact, it was the inertia driving her decisions. When Mrs. Breckinridge arrived in Kentucky, Appalachian women were three times more likely to die giving birth than women in the British Isles. To these people, childbirth was hazardous, and they accepted the doleful odds without lingering on it. If the mother gushed blood after the birth, they felt powerless to do anything but take hold of her clammy hand and pray her away to a proper Beyond as the life drained from her.

Mrs. Breckinridge explained to her nurses that mountain people naturally cherished their babies, and the arrival of a live one was the successful conclusion to the process. "They weren't considering the health and well-being of the *mothers*. If a mother began the labor process already weakened, they accepted that her chances of surviving were not good. Our emphasis will be on pre-natal care to reverse the factors causing mothers to waste away and die."

Granny midwives were resourceful. They contrived their mysterious medicinals from the wilds around their homes. Remedies had been passed down for generations, and those the white settlers didn't know of, they learned from the Indians' aboriginal cures. To bolster their remedies they added superstitions. A sharpened axe placed under the bed, bit-side up, was supposed to cut the pain and fever of childbirth. To ward off a miscarriage, the granny would make tea from black gum bark and sweet apple tree bark that she had peeled one piece up and one piece down.

Granny midwives' qualifications were earned from experience rather than book learning. One was known to own a doctor book, but she could not read. She used the illustrations as her guide. "We knew of one granny who could not read or count, so she kept track of each birth by adding a knot to a ball of string," Mrs. Breckinridge said. The granny's tools were basic: a knife or scissors to cut the baby's umbilical cord, a supply of lard, and a flask of whiskey – presumably for the mother. If labor was slow to start, the granny would give the woman gunpowder "to start the miseries." To soothe the pain, grannies gave ginger tea, white oak bark tea, and quinine. More than one granny swore that drinking chimney soot dissolved in hot water helped. The newborn's first drink might be catnip tea.

"You've got to respect someone whom the locals name their baby girls after," Mrs. Breckinridge observed, "but I'm ever skeptical of the unregistered, itinerant opportunists who call themselves 'doctor.' One of these charlatans regularly did *not* show up for the deliveries, therefore *saving* untold numbers of lives."

Even though the grannies were respected, trusted, and held in high regard, something was missing, and Mrs. Breckinridge knew what it was.

The success of the British system began with scheduled care during pregnancy. A medically-trained nurse attended the birth, which was followed by a series of post-partum checkups. Mrs. Breckinridge made this the cornerstone of her nursing service. As eager as she was to unseat the ineffective folk methods, she paced her plan to earn trust first, then enlist help to spread the mission. "When you invite yourself to a country where they plant potatoes and nail down their shingles according to the cycles of the moon, you've got to go slowly bringing laboratory-tested medicine into their lives," Mrs. Breckinridge said.

While construction was underway on the six outpost nursing centers, the FNS founder turned her energies to recruiting graduate nurse-midwives to staff them. This was truly a pioneering step because there were none on her own continent. She turned to the British Isles, and recruited experienced nurse-midwives she had met during her own time abroad.

"Our tasks are really two-fold," she would exclaim during her fund-raising speeches beyond the mountains, "We need to train staff and get them into our outpost clinic areas, all the while gently persuading the locals to allow us to begin helping enlighten them... to put aside for good the old folk methods of gunpowder, whiskey, and that abominable axe under the bed!"

In 1928, the first nurse-midwives in the United States were the sixteen she had recruited for the FNS staff. At first the locals were put off by the imported English nurses' "fotched-on ways" of wearing pants and riding horses straddle-wise. Soon, their sincerity and the funny way they said things endeared them to the people. Naturally, there was a pocket of resentment here and there, but Mrs. Breckinridge was a gifted organizer who knew it was important to give folks the feeling they were moving along of their own volition.

"That old gray mare's got a way o' pushin' people from the front," one granny complained. "She comes 'round here big-like and I would leaver she didn't put her nose in our bizness but I know her heart's in the right place."

Mary Breckinridge visualized a school of midwifery, to train professional nurse-midwives. This would add to the family practice and public nursing that her corps of nurses was bringing to ten thousand people. She knew she needed to serve pregnant women in their homes, rather than expect them to come to the new twelve-bed hospital in Hyden.

The Frontier Graduate School of Midwifery, staffed with trained nurse-midwives from England, was established so the success of the British approach could take root in the United States. Together, they created curriculum and on November 1, 1939, classes began for the six-month semester. Two American nurses enrolled in this first class. It was the first such school to endure on the American continent.

"Upon the arrival of a new 'least one,' so naked and helpless, it's easy to overlook that a full-term newborn is likely the healthiest soul in the birthing room," she said, "but it is a critical crossroad in the life of the mother. With our training, we are better prepared to address the most common threats to the health of the mother: toxemia and hemorrhaging." Toxemia (or pre-eclampsia) was usually a result of poor nutrition during pregnancy, and hemorrhaging could occur after the birth. Both of these killers were preventable, as the Frontier Nursing Service proved since its founding.

"Reliable statistics were essential to the success of the Frontier Nursing Service," Mrs. Breckinridge said. "It was the only way to survey results and make improvements where needed." She set up a simple but exacting system to record births. "Our nurses would not be making notches in wood, nor knotting string to keep track," she concluded.

In September 1939, the shadow of war crossed the Atlantic. When Britain declared war on Germany, Mrs. Breckinridge was staying with friends in Lexington during a fundraising trip. "I realized during a British radio broadcast that the war had already affected us," she later recalled. "I could hear the gravity of Britain's situation in Mr. Churchill's voice." Indeed, she was right. World War II brought a sea-change to the FNS. The British midwives she depended on for post-graduate training sensed a growing need to return to their home country. By the middle of 1940, several returned to England after learning of the London bombings. Some remained to finish out the semester of training, but soon the FNS lost eleven of the twenty-eight British nurse-midwives.

Her staff was straining to cover all its commitments to the community: Bedside nursing, staffing its six outpost nursing centers, public health, pre-natal and post-partum care and an abounding crop of babies. Other problems nagged the service. Fundraising was more difficult, with the nation turning its concern toward a tragedy as big as war. The FNS had to be even more shrewd with resources –cash, commodities and staff.

Who's Left To Fight A Fire?

"*T*his blasted war is taking all the men out of here, and their scarcity is most inconvenient," British nurse-midwife Cherry Evans lamented to Donna, as she dropped, exhausted, onto a chair and tossed her scuffed and dirty riding boots aside.

After the surprise attack on Pearl Harbor on December 7, 1941, many of the young men left Kentucky to enlist in the military; others chose to answer the patriotic call to work beyond the Cumberlands in industries that served the war effort. Men who remained in the area and who were working in the coal mines had their workload increased to a six-day week. Able-bodied men were indeed scarce.

It was Saturday afternoon. Nurses alternated weekends off, and Cherry had ridden to Hyden for the rest of the weekend to take a break and exchange news with Donna and the other nurses. After catching her breath she launched into the story of the house fire while she was on district, and how she and the neighbor lady were the only ones around to deal with it.

She had departed Confluence for her rounds, including a routine post-partum visit on a mother and two-week-old baby. When she arrived at the home, the family was gone neighboring briefly for a Christmas visit. A kind neighbor woman was staying at the home until the family returned. It was a damp, cold day along the river, and inside the cabin the little fire was barely keeping the cold away from itself. It seemed harmless, but there must have been some green firewood smoldering in the open fireplace. There was a "pop" and within seconds the old brittle newspaper lining the walls of the place started afire.

"You'd be amazed how fast the flames raced up the wall to the ceiling," Cherry told them. "We threw all the water we could find at the flames, then we grabbed a pot and an empty lard can and ran outside to fetch more." The quick-thinking woman stowed the can of lard and a kerosene can outside on her way to the river. They climbed on chairs and the bed to dowse the ceiling.

"We had trouble seeing, and the air was beginning to choke us," she said, "then we decided to strip off what newspaper we could, to try to limit the fire." Their strategy worked, and among the choking smoke, steam, sooty water and soggy newspaper flung about, they rejoiced that they'd saved the home.

"With the wood fires and lamps, cooking grease stored everywhere, and children running about in the small rooms, it's a wonder there aren't more fires!" a nurse exclaimed. Donna and the others agreed.

Their rejoicing was short-lived however. Two weeks after this near-tragedy the Wendover staff was at lunch in the big house when a neighbor ran up the path yelling, "FIRE! THE LOWER BUILDING IS ON *FIRE!*" Everyone jumped up from the table. The couriers ran to the barn to move the horses before they panicked and bolted. The others headed to the coils of fire hose stored on the premises or dashed about to get other tools. The Garden House – the administration office of the FNS and Wendover dormitory – had caught fire.

At the time, Ellery was at one of the outposts on his horseshoeing round.

There were so few men around, that it was mostly up to the nurses and staff to do a fire department's job. They hauled out and connected the fire hoses, tapping into the big cistern above the buildings, and handled the heavy hoses trying to save the building. The bookkeeper, Lucile Hodges, heroically crawled inside beneath the dense pall of smoke, and from the main office window, tossed drawers of important papers to safety below. When the fire began to consume the painstakingly-kept records, she was forced to escape the building. Hopeless about saving the Garden House, the women turned the hose on the next-closest building, the big oak barn, and started wetting it down. By now, the couriers had moved the horses and other livestock to a safe place alongside the river and were doing their best to calm the frightened animals. Mrs. Breckinridge had had the foresight to space the Wendover structures far apart to minimize fire risk. She had specified fire-resistant shingles on all the two-story buildings, but these precautions were of little relief. The building burned to its stone foundation before their eyes on that cold January day in 1942.

Garden House fire January, 1942 — *courtesy of FNS.*

Chimney fires were a persistent danger, and it was Mrs. Breckinridge's unwavering policy that all chimneys be regularly cleaned and checked. No one anticipated that the building's coal-burning furnace might be overstrained trying to handle the cold snap.

The insurance company paid out five thousand dollars. After news of the loss was publicized, people from all over the nation responded with cash gifts, some of them very large. The generous response amazed Mrs. Breckinridge, as it was totally unsolicited. The funds enabled the FNS to build a larger structure, better accommodating the offices and dormitory. There was enough money to partly furnish it. New Pyrene fire extinguishers about the size of a metal thermos bottle were installed throughout.

The outpouring of support went a long way to ease the sense of loss over the demise of the lovely building.

News traveled quickly that the staff who were stationed there at the time of the fire lost all their personal possessions. Soon boxes of clothes began arriving from thoughtful people and organizations. Local folks who had very little to share did their best to reciprocate for all the kindnesses the nurses had shown them. They brought things they thought the women would find useful: home-made soap, quilts and cane-bottom chairs. More than one family handed over their most cherished linens which could be turned into curtains, and one family sacrificed their hand-held mirror.

As she gathered up the gifts the locals had brought, Lucile spotted the mirror with its beautiful hand-made polished wooden handle. "Not to diminish the value of the donations from our patrons . . ." she privately remarked to Mrs. Breckinridge, "but in ratio to their ability to give, these treasures are far and beyond all the other gifts combined."

The Outpost Center

*A*ny time of the day or night a Frontier nurse could get a "hurry call" for someone up Greasy Creek, Cut Shin, Devil's Jump, Danger Branch of Bullskin Creek, Big Bear Branch or some other unobliging-sounding place. There was Still House Hollow, Buzzard Roost and Deep Gap. Donna was expected to know how to get there quickly. Often she was called out at what was poetically called "the edge of dark," knowing that most of the ride through the close-in hollows would be "after good dark had come on."

Being new to the territory, Donna sometimes asked for directions. The reply went something like this: "Cross the swingin' bridge and go upriver till you hit Hog Wallow Fork. Be mindful o' the quicksand there. Go upstream o' that to where it sort o' levels out. Keep a'goin' till you see a wasp nest at the edge o' the hackberry. Keep the rock outcrop above you and foller the hog path a ways; you'll happen on an old beech tree. Keep a'goin' a piece. Cross one branch, and look up the hill, and you'll see our place. If you hit a second branch, you've passed us by."

Kentucky has more miles of running waterways than all the states except Alaska. It was usually best to follow a drainage to find your way. "North, south, east and west" are abstract notions that had no meaning in this country. It didn't matter which direction the creek twisted and tumbled, you could always count on it heading one direction – down. If you thought you'd lost your way, you'd go downstream and you would end up someplace you recognized – eventually.

Each outpost served about eighty square miles, if you wanted to figure it that way. But there are no "square miles" in southeastern Kentucky. The terrain is rumpled and steep, and once you leave the bottom land there are few roads.

The region hadn't seen many neighborhood improvements. Few places had electricity when Donna arrived, and there were no telephones. The homes were scattered with no city water or sewer system. For generations, people had used dug-wells and outhouses – usually situated too close to each other.

The only farmable land in this passed-by country was along the rivers, and they overran their banks nearly every spring. The water was, as Mark Twain said, "too thick to drink and too thin to plow." The hardy soul who staked out a life here had to be well-suited to hardship. Pioneer settlers brought their fierce, clannish Scots-Irish ways, honed by centuries of enduring in the rocky, wind-blown latitudes of the northern British Isles.

Mrs. Breckinridge called it "a place where milk comes from one thousand different cows, many with Bangs disease; and the water supply comes from a thousand wells and springs, many of them infected. Family sewage is not carried off and disposed of by sanitary engineers. It contaminates his environment." This was her way of saying there was lots of illness to stamp out and a lifetime of education to spread.

Every nurse starting out with the Frontier Nursing Service was assigned "floater" duty – Mrs. Breckinridge's way of acquainting her with the entire service area. Donna would complete a circuit of all the centers, serving with the senior nurse in residence who would familiarize her with the facility, the families and the trails. At the end of her first circuit, she was expected to be competent with the system's methods. She was then assigned to an outpost as a more permanent resident nurse along with a senior nurse. At this point, she could make home visits and staff the clinic alone if her senior nurse was on a midwifery case – a delivery.

The nurses were sitting together for the evening meal at the dorm at Hyden. Donna was happy to catch up with Evelyn, who had already spent a month as a floater. She was adding entertaining stories to the table chatter.

"I think I saw a moonshiner," she said between mouthfuls of mashed potatoes and chicken gravy. "I was tempted to stop and look for his still. He just watched me pass by on the trail. He was holding a gun!"

After dinner, Evelyn confided to Donna that one day at Wendover, as she was getting ready to ride to Flat Creek for duty, Mrs. Breckinridge walked down the path toward the barn. "I thought she was on her way past me, but she stopped right there by Rusty and me and smiled." Evelyn paused. "She has this sixth sense. Then she asked if I'd cleaned my horse's hooves yet. And I hadn't. I don't like that smelly job. Especially Rusty's back hooves.

" 'Isn't that the couriers' job?' I asked. What a mistake! I should have just admitted that I hadn't. She scolded me like you wouldn't believe. She didn't cuss, but she might as well have. I felt terrible."

The next morning Donna was to begin her floater duty at Beech Fork clinic and join Nancy, the senior nurse-midwife. After breakfast, she carried her saddlebags and a rucksack of personal effects out of the dormitory. Winter was making a final sweep over Thousandsticks before its final retreat. Two saddled horses stood in front of the sixteen-stall Hyden barn, their breath making soft clouds in the crisp air.

"Mornin', Miz Donna," Ellery said in his gentle voice. "This here's Jefferson. I know you axed fer a low-heighted horse, but this here gelding's as gentle as flannel cake. If you c'n figger out how to get on him, I'll bound he'll let you stay there as long as you like."

He took her saddlebags and slung them over the saddle, and showed Donna how to secure them. He fastened her personal bag behind his saddle. Ellery would accompany her to Beech Fork, and check the condition of the horses there before returning. He always carried a satchel of farriers' tools in case a horseshoe repair was needed.

Taking a long, slow breath, Donna approached the animal and stroked his neck to get acquainted.

"Good morning, Jefferson," she said, with forced confidence, masking the apprehension she felt in her gut. She had to trust Ellery's judgment of the animal. "No doubt he knows the animal's ability, but he hasn't an inkling about mine," she thought. The horse had a beautiful head and bright eyes with no hint of malice. His long winter hair was a dull, dark brown. While she hesitated, Ellery stepped over and thoughtfully unbuckled and lengthened the left stirrup strap to make it easier for her to reach. He discreetly stepped back to hold the bridle, so as not to view Donna's backside as she prepared to mount. She grasped the stirrup, and placing the ball of her left foot in it, she bounced three or four times on her right foot then leapt up. The plantation endurance-style saddle had no horn, but the pommel made for a pretty solid handle. She surprised herself by mounting the horse in one try. It was graceless, but she was on.

Ellery couldn't hide his broad smile, and Donna noticed how it made his whole face light up in an agreeable way. They both looked back down at the horse. Ellery stepped close to her left leg and showed her how to re-adjust the stirrup to a comfortable length for riding.

"Ellery, I believe the hardest part of my day is now over," she said, and didn't mind admitting to him that she had been anxious about this moment. She was comfortable around the horseshoer, and began looking forward to their ride together.

They rode down into Hyden, a village of mismatched structures resting in skewed positions where Rockhouse Creek joins the Middle Fork of the Kentucky River. Folks they saw nodded or waved at the two riders.

It was about sixteen miles to the outpost clinic, mostly good going along the river. Donna felt a glow of growing confidence, with Ellery alongside her on this first horseback outing. Her horse had a smooth walking gait, and never spooked at little disturbances like the lemon-sized stone that rolled across their path from the embankment above. He seemed very sure-footed, even when they crossed the icy creeks. By eleven o'clock they had arrived. Donna immediately felt at home, seeing the whitewashed center for the first time. It sat well above the creek, and had a certain dignity to it. Calico curtains flanked the clean glass windows which let in lots of morning light. The large garden spot lying dormant in a sunny clearing reminded her of home.

Like each of the outpost nursing centers, Beech Fork was a combination clinic and residence. The clinic section had a gambrel roof with windowed gables, letting in more sunshine. The living quarters had a cross-gable roof, covered porch and windows with cheerful green shutters. The two of them rode up to the hitching post and Donna dismounted, steadying herself a moment while Ellery released her luggage and set it down for her. He took the horses to the barn and Donna entered the clinic side.

Nancy greeted her and began showing her around. It was clean and serviceable, but primitive compared to the operating room where Donna had worked in Petoskey. She could smell a blend of Lysol and coal-oil, and a hint of baking cornbread. The large waiting room had cane-bottom chairs along one wall, a cot and a crib with a screen surrounding it to keep insects out. Nancy showed Donna the dispensary, and the record-keeping box with a folder for each family.

"You can take some time and look over our records," she said. "You'll find names of each family member, the condition of their homes, and most important, their water supply and privy – and where their water supply is in relation to their barn, pigpen or chicken coop. We like to learn about their milk supply, too, if there are children. Our 'natals' are all booked in there too, in a separate section." Donna started to peer into the collection of tidy papers. Nancy took her arm and said warmly, "But come on, I'll show you your room now."

In front of the fireplace in the residence's main room were two overstuffed chairs and a shelf of books, mostly related to nursing and medicine. There were a few novels for an easy-chair escape from the job. Donna's bedroom had a twin bed covered with a handmade quilt, a small writing table and chair, and kerosene lamps.

Beechfork Nursing Center, 2009 – *Author photo.*

A man and a young boy came in the clinic entrance, and hesitated a moment on its battleship gray linoleum floor.

"Good morning, fellows, come in and meet Donna, our new nurse." The boy's left hand had been neatly bandaged, but was brown-gray from a week of being on the end of a busy mountain boy's arm.

"This is Clarence, and the little soldier with the battle wound is Wendel."

"I'm pleased to meet you both," Donna said.

"I'm good-pleased to meet you, miss," Clarence said, removing his hat. Wendel looked up and smiled, revealing new front teeth that were outsized for his young face.

"Let's take a look at your cut, Wendel. I think I can get rid of those pesky stitches for you today." Nancy unwrapped the dingy gauze while the boy looked shyly from one woman to the other.

"You've healed up nicely, Wendel. Now, next time you try to cut up a lard can, please wear gloves."

Turning to Donna, she said, "He was trying to make a sled for his little sister. The sheet metal took a pretty big slice out of his thenar. He missed the tendon, thank the good Lord," she added quietly.

Throughout the day, the nurses took care of a dozen or more walk-ins. There were burns to examine and re-dress; a man came to get more medicine for his wife, who suffered from pellagra.

"She's mendin' well. She takes her nourishment now without squanderin' herself," he told Nancy.

"I'm very glad Ellen's diarrhea has stopped," Nancy said, to translate for Donna, "that is a good sign, Branley."

There was an axe injury to clean and suture. A woman brought in a child who'd stepped on a nail. A man came in with a jagged splinter in the back of his head from a rough timber that flipped while he was hoisting it over his head. "I was surprised he didn't try to dig it out himself with a dirty jackknife," Nancy said after he left. "Then in a week, we'd be treating him for blood poisoning."

Once or twice a week, the nurses would ride out for a day "on-district." They planned these circuits, giving priority to their expectant mothers. Other visits had to fit around those calls. The nurses usually left early, stopping in at as many homes as they could. They tried to return to the center by dark.

Nurses wore watches, since a timepiece was useful for timing a woman's labor pains. But out on district, the hour was signaled by the light in the sky. Folks in the hollows followed a three-part rhythm: day was for milking, planting, hoeing or harvesting; night was when babies were born; and in-between was the edge of dark, for the evening milking and bringing the chickens in to keep them safe from varmints.

"I can count on one hand the number of times I actually came through our gate before dark," Nancy explained. "You get used to working the 'red-eye shift' because that's when you catch up on record-keeping."

In order to reach the remotest families, the nurses held clinic days at locations at the outskirts of their district. They used a schoolhouse or one of the small, non-residential FNS buildings for vaccines or clinical checkups. If someone needed treatment beyond what the nurses could do, the person was referred to the Hyden Hospital, where the only doctor within fifty miles practiced. If the person could travel, they would make the trip by mule or horseback. Rarely was it practical to use a vehicle. What roads there were, treacherously followed the creek bottoms, which were usually impassable. If the patient's condition was too critical, the doctor would be called to the outpost – unless an infected appendix was suspected. Folks tended to ignore a stomach ache until it hurt so bad it bent them over in pain. By the time help was summoned, the nurses had to push the realm of possibility to get the sufferer into Hyden for emergency surgery before it ruptured.

Transporting injured patient across the Middle Fork
of the Kentucky — *FNS photo by Marvin Breckinridge
Patterson, courtesy of Univ. of Kentucky archives.*

Nurse gives a "field vaccine" out on district
— *Reid family photo.*

Telephone lines had been strung along the Middle Fork, but only Confluence Center had a connection to Hyden. Nancy explained the complicated telephone procedure to Donna. "When we, Flat Creek, Brutus or Red Bird need to contact Hyden hospital, we ring up the exchange at Bowlingtown. Bowlingtown telephones Confluence, who telephones it to the Hyden exchange. They call the hospital to talk to the doctor. You'll think you are talking to someone on the other side of the world."

Nancy and Donna closed the clinic for the evening and enjoyed a hot meal of ham, cornbread and pickles that their housekeeper had prepared before she went home. After eating, Donna began reviewing the records and the two nurses chatted about them over cups of tea.

"I see children that have been treated for worms several times," Donna commented.

"It's a seasonal thing here," Nancy replied. "When barefoot weather comes, we'll start seeing more worm cases. It's as regular as dogwood."

"A long cold winter, and we see more tuberculosis, because of the close indoor conditions," Nancy continued. "There's always typhoid. You probably saw several skin lesions in the files. Poor winter diet leads to pellagra and gallbladder trouble. There's a long spell after they use up their fall harvest and before the coming on of fresh greens. That's when they suffer the most. Poor diet really increases toxemia in our pregnant women, too."

Donna sipped her tea thoughtfully. She was beginning to feel overwhelmed.

"But the saddest cases we see are the children who get burned. Frontier kitchens are a maze of hazards for the little ones. And children spend a lot of time with no supervision. During canning or molasses season . . . little girls' cotton dress sleeves catch fire over the stoves . . . Oh, Donna, I shouldn't overwhelm you just now with all that. You must be tired."

Donna had a hard time thinking of sleep with the family records jammed in her mind, so she decided to write home. The lamps lit up her cozy room. She noticed ice crystals beginning to form on the window. She was grateful for the braided rag rugs that kept her feet off the hardwood floor. Propping herself up with the feather bolster in her warm bed, she wrote:

> *Dearest ones,*
> *I've begun duty at Beech Fork, my first outpost clinic. It's called Floater duty, but after my day in the saddle I'm calling it Flopper duty. I'll be working from all six outposts so that I learn our whole territory.*
>
> *Ellery the nice horseshoer got me a gentle horse, but he's taller than old Sandy. His name is Jefferson for Mrs. B's cousin who donates a lot to the FNS. We've engineered a way I can get on him easier by lowering a stirrup. After riding a dozen miles, I had to convince my legs to straighten back out for walking. I'll be here a couple of weeks working with Nancy the senior nurse, but she's my age. There's plenty to do. There are about 250 families to serve from here.*
>
> *Beech Fork is beautiful. It has a large garden. Around here they raise corn, beans, cushaw squash and canning vegetables. Ellery said they raise the best tomatoes I'll ever eat, but I made a friendly bet with him that our Burt Lake tomatoes are better!*
>
> *Tomorrow we work in this clinic – then we'll go out on district where we make house calls on horseback.*
>
> *Love, D*
> *PS: Please send me some tomato and watermelon seeds.*

She always felt better after she wrote home. Her tone of confidence was a little hollow, but she didn't want her family to worry about her. She twisted the knurled knobs to snuff the lamps, and lay in the dark feeling little of the self-assurance she possessed during her days in the surgical room at Petoskey. Mrs. Breckinridge sort of gave you big orders then went on to other things. "Maybe when I meet more local people I'll gain more confidence," she thought. They seemed grateful that you were there, even though they were shy.

Spring Blooms and Other Surprises

"*E*llery, I will be riding solo to the Confluence center at Possum Bend tomorrow morning, and I've never ridden there by myself," Donna said to the kind horseshoer. She was happy to be back at Wendover for the afternoon because it gave her a chance to talk with him. As much as she enjoyed a meal or tea with Mrs. Breckinridge and other nurses in the big house, she was more comfortable outside watching Ellery work. This time she especially wanted his advice before she set out alone for the twelve-mile ride down the Middle Fork. It was easy to talk to Ellery. He never made you feel like you'd just asked a dumb question.

Donna had completed a circuit, working at the six outpost centers, and was now assigned to the Confluence outpost for a longer period. She had only been there once and that was with a courier who rode with her from the Bowlingtown outpost. Donna had never ridden out to Confluence from Hyden, and she'd heard there was quicksand in the river area.

"Sure, Miz Donna. Jus' foller the Middle Fork downstream past Bull Creek . . . past Cut Shin . . . past Hell-fer-Certain . . . the land'l level out and the river's gonna make an oxbow to the right. Jefferson's given over to the way there. Once't he knows where yer headed, he'll take you right to the barn."

"What about quicksand, Ellery?"

"You get quicksand at the mouth of the branches after a tide. I misdoubt you'll happen onto any tomorrow."

"Tide?" questioned Donna.

"Yup. You can count on a tide whenever they's a frog-strangler."

Donna puzzled over that for a second, then realized he meant heavy rain. "Rain enough to flood?"

"We say 'flood' only when it's a big enough tide to rearrange the buildings and swamp out the garden goods," he explained. "Tides is part of *life* here. Floods is part of . . . well . . . *not* life."

She understood. The way he looked at her always made her feel less of an outsider.

"You never ferget that look in an animal's eyes while they're gettin' swallowed up in a flood, and there's nothin' you c'n do to save 'em." He looked down and jammed his hands in his pockets. They stood still a moment in shared silence. He broke the stillness by stepping over to pick up an old newspaper, to prepare his forge fire for the next day's work.

Spring's first warm sun had brought a bee out of its winter stupor, and they heard it pelting the inside of one of the barn windows. Ellery, with the newspaper still in one hand, located the bee and opened the window, cupped his free hand and gently scooped it outside.

"We don't want to keep this little feller from doin' his bizness," he said, charming Donna with his tenderness.

It was time to join the others in the big house for dinner.

Donna said goodbye. She'd been hoping Ellery might have some reason to go to Possum Bend to check on a horse or something. She realized it was silly to think that he might offer to ride with her in the morning. Of course he had things to do here at Wendover. Donna made her way up to the big house along the blossom path that was planted in terraces on the steep, partially-sunny side hill. Pink and lavender blooms were appearing between the stones, and the face-powder smell of peonies reminded her of her yard in Michigan. The flute-like phrase of a wood thrush came from the direction of the eaves.

The women were already in the front room. When Donna entered she was offered tea or a glass of sherry. Mrs. Breckinridge greeted her warmly. From where Donna sat, she could see the Middle Fork through the leaves that were beginning to bud out on the beech tree in front of the big house. She sipped her tea and wondered if the maple trees at home were also starting to show spring growth.

Mrs. Breckinridge told the others that Donna was going to Confluence in the morning to staff the outpost with Rosie. "Be mindful not to sound patronizing," she told Donna. "We must respect the dignity of our families, no matter their status or conditions in which they live."

Donna had already observed some of those conditions. She had treated a patient for anemia in a home with a packed dirt floor and no windows. Snakes or rodents could easily have found their way in, between the crude wall boards and the floor. She'd walked past a bloody butchering stump to get to the place, and bumped her head on a skinned animal carcass hanging from the porch stringer.

"Do not be timid about accepting payment. It's wise to carry along a feed sack. It will make it easier to bring the payment back to the clinic if it comes in the form of a live chicken or goose." Although her eyes twinkled, Mrs. Breckinridge did not mean this as a joke.

"Until you are a trained *midwife*, naturally you'll be serving with a nurse who has completed training. Hopefully your pre-natals will not surprise you with an emergency delivery while the nurse-midwife is already away delivering someone else!"

Donna was considering that possibility when Mrs. Breckinridge continued, "And my dear, you have already shown excellent common sense and revealed your kind heart. Kindness, especially around the children, is an important counterpoint to the 'infant damnation' messages of the severely religious. As we spread our service and compassion, perhaps the next generation will abandon that cruel doctrine. If they wish, let the family pray fervently over your patient as you work. It certainly doesn't hurt to invite the good Lord into the room."

The hearty meal was served, and as usual there was spirited conversation between the staff and Mrs. Breckinridge. There was canned cherry pie for dessert. For Donna, the best part came after the meal. Ardice excused herself and left the dining room. In a moment, they heard paws skittering on the hardwood floor and Ardice reappeared at the trailing end of a leash. A middle-size, long-haired black and white dog with beautiful brown eyes began making quick acquaintances around the table. "Donna, we named him 'Buckeye' to honor one of our Cincinnati patrons and because his eyes are pretty as chestnuts!" Ardice had to speak over the friendly commotion. "I'm afraid he is of questionable pedigree. He was dumped off near here, but at least he knows the country better than an imported purebred. I hope you like him!"

Donna knelt down, her face broke into a wide grin, and with both hands she scratched the dog behind his ears. He was a muddled cross of breeds. He loved her touch and sat, with what could only have been his own wide grin. Donna's usual terseness gave way to delight. "I'm sure we'll get along just fine," she said, a chuckle in her voice. "I wouldn't want one that's too good for daily wear."

Donna was up and dressed before daylight reached the east side of the dorm building. By flashlight, with Buckeye right beside her, she walked to the barn to feed Jefferson. A whip-poor-will called from the woods above the buildings. She returned to the dorm and heated some cereal for breakfast, and packed a sandwich before leaving.

The dog trotted a length or two ahead of her horse. Jefferson didn't seem to mind their new companion, and Donna was pleased to have the extra set of ears. Jefferson was usually the first to sense something out of the ordinary along the trail but Donna knew the dog could offer a little different perspective on a situation. He could help her sort out the trifles from the troubles. The horse wasn't quite that intellectual.

Jefferson had shed his dull, long winter hair and was a shiny dark brown, the color of oil-polished walnut wood. His head bobbed rhythmically as he put the horseback miles behind them. He never shied when they flushed out a nesting Kentucky warbler from the brush near the trail.

Springtime in this country surprised you every day with a new bloom. Sassafras and alder trees were daubing the gray woods with new color. Serviceberry was the first to blossom out, followed by redbud and dogwood. Donna was enchanted by the display of redbud, a tree that explodes into a red-purple corona of color. She had never seen the tropical-looking big-leaf magnolia, with its yellow-white blossoms. Later blackberry would bloom, then the wild rhododendron. Closer to the ground, beneath spring's waking underbrush you might spot the delicate trillium.

The land leveled and opened out. She saw a bend in the river and stopped the horse. Donna wondered if it was the right "oxbow"

Ellery had mentioned. Jefferson pulled against the reins trying to graze. She let him nuzzle and clip at the little grasses while she tried to recall Ellery's directions. Buckeye sat and looked up at her. By now, Jefferson seemed content with his grazing and Donna feared he might not be such a reliable compass to the nursing center barn. She was about to chance the next leg of her trip when Buckeye stood, tensed, and turned to face the trail behind them. Donna heard the sound just as Ellery emerged on horseback. She inhaled with a little thrill as she waited for him.

"After you lit out, Miz Donna, I rec'llected I needed to check on some busted hardware up to Confluence," he said to her, quickly looking in the direction of the center. "Thank you fer holdin' up fer me."

Ellery passed her and Donna nudged Jefferson to follow, enjoying a warm sense of security as she fixed her eyes on his familiar hat.

Song sparrows piped their joy and a mourning dove added rueful tones as they approached their destination. The cheerful white two-story outpost looked over the Middle Fork from its setting high above the threat of flood. Striped awnings over each window gave it a friendly look.

Arriving at the nursing center, Ellery took charge of the horses and told her he'd be returning to Wendover shortly.

"Not until I pack you a sandwich to take with you," she said.

"I'd be much obliged Miz Donna," he said, flashing his fetching smile at her before he disappeared into the barn.

Donna hurried into the building and washed up to help Rosie.

Another surprise Spring brought was intestinal parasites. Just as Nancy had warned her, the cases of worms were showing up. Donna's only exposure to them had been in a medical textbook.

"He's feeling puny," complained the young mother when it was her little boy's turn. Donna had the youngster sit on her lap and tell her how he was feeling. He looked peaked and listless.

"I'd like to a' died – I was a'sweatin' all over. My belly hurt so bad and I couldn't get my breath." His mother explained that his grandmother had given him Black Draught, which Donna knew was a drugstore laxative. "But you c'n see he's still poorly," she added.

"I lost my stommick fer eatin' when I see'd them little worms," the boy said, "then they come out some big fishin' worms."

Donna tried not to act shocked. The little fellow was so earnest.

The family took their water from a spring, and had no deep privy. Donna discussed this problem with the mother. Now that the child was infected, the treatment would be a "one-two punch" of santonin and calomel. The santonin killed or immobilized intestinal parasites, and the mercury-based calomel acted as a purgative to rid the body of the stunned invaders. Donna had the boy swallow the first pill with lots of the clinic's pure well water. She gave the mother clear instructions that he not eat breakfast in the morning. The family was to drink only water that had been boiled. Donna said she'd bring the second pill to her in the morning, and check the boy.

"I'll be sure to see where they pen up their livestock," thought Donna. "It's very likely uphill from where they draw their water." This would explain the problem. Chicken coops, hog pens, barns and privies needed to be far enough away from the supply of domestic water to keep the families from continually getting infected.

"Talking things over"— *Earl Palmer photo, from FNS Quarterly Bulletin.*

The last patient of the day was an eleven-year-old boy who had been losing weight in spite of his enormous appetite. The previous spring he had been sent to Hyden Hospital with what turned out to be diabetes. Now he was languishing with nausea and blurry vision. Fearing his illness was returning, his mother brought him in. Rosie explained to Donna that this family provided for themselves better than most, so nutrition was not the cause of his diabetes. Donna suspected a culprit. She thought out her question carefully.

"Delmer, *how often* do you chew tobacco?"

"Miss Donna, I chew it ever' day."

"What kind do you chew?" she asked.

"I like our own patch 'baccer best, but when ours runs out, Daddy lets me chew plug 'baccer from town."

Donna knew that store-bought tobacco was sweetened, and because the boy chewed so much, the evidence pointed to a dietary imbalance from all the sweetener – which would explain the seasonal timing of his illness.

"Delmer, I know you don't want to get sick again like last year."

"No, ma'am. I'd be much pleased to not be sick again."

"I'm going to give you two choices that might keep you from getting sick. You must promise me to do one or the other for us. Is it a deal?"

"Yes'm. I give my word."

"Stop using tobacco altogether . . . or you only use tobacco that does *not* come from the store."

The nurses promised to visit on their next on-district day. The boy knelt down beside Buckeye, who was lying by the clinic door. He petted the dog, and reluctantly left the clinic when his mother insisted.

When the day was over, Donna fed and watered Buckeye. When he finished eating, she rubbed his clean white chest and found his favorite scratching spots. He needed a nickname. "Bucky" she thought. The simple name fit. The dog sensed how happy Donna was. He found a place he liked on the braided rug, circled a few times, then lay down as Donna began unpacking.

She brought with her a few longer-stay luxuries. As she placed her packet of writing paper and envelopes on the writing table, a dog-eared newspaper clipping slipped out. It was the Frontier Nursing Service advertisement from the *Petoskey News-Review*. She had forgotten all about it. It seemed so long ago that she and Evelyn sat together in that Michigan hospital and first saw the offer. The job wasn't very much like the "summer camp" Evelyn had imagined, but if the FNS promised you something they came through with it. Sure enough, Donna now had her own horse and her own dog. All that was left was the "thousand miles of Kentucky mountains to serve." She had no doubt that promise would also come true.

She wondered what surprises the rest of the locals would have for her. She'd been trained in a spotless, well-lighted atmosphere with every modern medical appliance at the ready. In this job, you never knew what conditions you'd encounter. There was no electricity, and at night, the kerosene lamp light was either smack in your eyes, or you were working in your own shadow.

An outward sense of confidence – even if it didn't reach to your core – helped put your patients at ease which always made nursing easier. If something was easy for you, it raised your confidence. It was a cycle you had to start yourself.

Working alongside Rosie – a graduate midwife who'd been here awhile – was comforting. And with the little Hyden hospital as part of the organization, she could refer patients she couldn't help. By now, most people were pretty accepting of the nurses' way of helping. They were very shy about examinations, but few of them balked at treatment. These days, it took almost no persuading to get the people to show up at clinics and bare their arms for diphtheria, smallpox and typhoid vaccines. Donna knew it had not always been that way for the nurses.

Her first night back at Possum Bend, Donna was feeling a little more settled with her personal belongings around her cozy bedroom. She knelt down by Bucky and stroked his head as he slept. He opened one eye long enough to express his gratitude and with a satisfied sigh, went back to sleep.

She took out paper and began writing:

> *Dearest ones,*
> *I hope you are enjoying spring as we are here. I saw redbud for the first time today. It is as beautiful as our cherry blossoms. It really surprised me with its sudden show of color. It's really more purple than red.*

Speaking of surprises, today we treated a child with . . . goodness! . . . roundworms. It was my first encounter, and I know it won't be the last. I'll do better next time a child describes what happens when his grandma tries to cure him with drug store laxatives.

We also saw a diabetic child today. Eleven years old. He gets too much sugar from guess what . . . store-bought chewing tobacco! He admitted to me that he chews every day. This did NOT surprise the mother. I tried not to show my surprise.

What next?

Love, D

PS: Don't worry about me. I'm at Confluence nursing center at Possum Bend and it is a very nice place to be. The most wonderful thing happened to me. Dicey gave me a beautiful dog I call Bucky. He makes me think of Patches. He'll be good company.

She thought of Ellery, but she resisted the urge to add anything about the kind and capable horseshoer.

Donna sealed the letter and got in bed. As she lay there, her thoughts turned to the previous evening at Wendover. She remembered Mrs. Breckinridge's exact words. She flicked on her flashlight, pulled the newspaper ad back out, and re-read it. Nowhere did it say anything about "midwife."

But Mrs. Breckinridge had definitely said, "Until you are a trained *midwife* . . ."

Now that was a surprise.

Graduate School

Donna was called back to Hyden after her short residency at the Confluence center at Possum Bend. She and Bucky arrived in time for dinner at the dormitory, and Evelyn was also there, bursting with news. "You are to see Miss Buck, too!" was all Evelyn said to her friend. Dorothy Buck was now Dean of the Frontier Graduate School of Midwifery.

"Good afternoon Donna," Miss Buck began. "As you know, we are earnestly trying to fill the void as our British women resign." Donna knew what she would be asked to do. It was obvious there was a shortage of nurse-midwives. The race was on to train new ones who could staff the clinics and eventually take on instructing duties. There was a sense of urgency to Miss Buck's side of the conversation. "Our own government has tripled its nurse training program and is sending American nurses to fifty countries." She continued on a more personal note. "Donna, you've proven your ability to serve in our unique circumstances. You know each center, its families and our procedures. We're 'escalating your training' as they say in the military."

Miss Buck offered Donna a scholarship to the school, meaning that within six months she'd be delivering babies on her own. As a floater, she'd worked alongside a senior nurse midwife on several deliveries already. She'd heard other nurses' stories of delivering babies in the dark, primitive cabins.

Donna read over the contract terms: six months of midwifery training and a pledge to stay with the FNS for a minimum of two years after completing her training. During the school term, her allowance would be $10 per month; room and board at the Hyden dorm would be provided. Once she graduated, her starting salary would be $100 a month, less forty dollars for board and laundry service. She would go where needed. Most likely that would be an outpost; or she might be needed at Hyden Hospital.

She accepted Miss Buck's terms to serve the FNS, but first she had to explain her personal situation. Her Michigan family had very humble means. They saw to the needs of one another. Her Aunt Myra had stepped right up to raise the three Carroll girls when their mother died. Donna and her twin sister were thirteen at the time, and the baby, only fourteen months old. Though widowed, Donna's aunt had managed to keep up the family farm, raise the motherless children, and provide a good life for them. When Donna decided to move out of state for this job, she assured Myra that she'd come back home to help if ever a family emergency might occur.

"We completely understand," Miss Buck said kindly. "Of course your family must be part of your decision." In a more somber tone she added, "there's a war on and babies to catch."

With a mix of excitement and heavy responsibility, Donna Elizabeth Carroll enrolled in the Frontier Graduate School of Midwifery and accepted the two-year minimum obligation. She could think of nothing more meaningful than a career with the FNS. Thoughts of home faded from Donna's mind.

At dinner that evening, the talk turned to delivering babies.

"I had a shoulder presentation way up above Red Bird," one of the nurses said. "I sent the husband to Red Bird center to have them call for the doctor at Hyden. I knew it would take a couple of hours for him to get to us. By the time he arrived, it seemed to me like it had been years!"

Everyone at the table agreed how the anxiety could build, but you couldn't show it.

"I sent for two neighbor women to help," the nurse continued. "The doctor and Miss Buck arrived, scrubbed, and we put out the fire in the fireplace and extinguished all the lamps so we could give the mother ether for anesthesia. The neighbor women supported the mother's legs. I snapped on the flashlight, Doctor reached in and rearranged the baby, and in a few minutes we had a healthy boy!"

So far, Donna had made rounds out on district with other nurses to the cabins in the areas. Pre-natal and post-partum visits were joyous moments; she was comfortable treating the various childhood afflictions in homes or at the clinic. Soon the responsibility of delivering babies would be hers. It was one thing to have a doctor nearby, and have a warm place, good lights, clean rooms and linens, hot and cold running water, and a staff to support you. But bringing a baby safely into the world, having seen the places where these babies caught their first breath, gave her pause.

"And with only what I can carry in a forty-pound saddlebag," she thought. "And not even a screen on the open windows, no indoor water . . . no light. Sometimes not even a privy . . ."

In bed that night, new doubts seized her. Nursing school back in Michigan was her greatest accomplishment up to now, and it had not been easy. Some of her classmates had dropped out; it was Donna's determination that had gotten her through. She laid awake a long time. She felt like she'd been handed a huge baton and told to run with it. She did not sleep well that night.

Saddlebag and Log Cabin Technique

"Place, on table in handy place, the bottle of Brandy."

— FNS "Setting up for delivery" instruction sheet

*D*onna and Evelyn were in the seventh class of the Frontier Graduate School of Midwifery. Class began in May, in the wood frame annex of the stone hospital building clinging to the hill above Hyden. Along with their four classmates, they would live in the compound on Thousandsticks Mountain for the next six months for intense training on how to deliver babies in all kinds of situations, including the "Saddlebag and Log Cabin Technique.[1] When they completed the semester, a doctor from the Kentucky Department of Health would conduct oral and written examinations and observe each student's practical work. If they passed, they could add "C.M." for "Certified Midwife" to the "R.N." behind their names.

Their instructor, Miss Gilbert, began by handing out the eleven-item Scoring Sheet for the nurses to study. Mrs. Breckinridge appeared in the classroom to cover the last item herself. It was titled "Driving Force."

"Students," she began, stepping beside the lectern, her clear blue eyes affixing on each woman in turn, "you must possess physical, intellectual and volitional energy for undertaking and completing your job. You must exhibit reliability of a type that gives your patients confidence you will not let them down, and you must have dependability of a quality that convinces supervisors you will bear without complaint or self-pity, your full share, *or more . . .* of

---

[1] Title of an article by Vanda Summers, RN, SCM, first published in *The American Journal of Nursing*, Nov., 1938 and reprinted in the FNS *Quarterly Bulletin*, Summer 1941.

the load of drudgery, labor and responsibility called for in your task at hand." It was her soul speaking. She'd repeated those words to each class before them. Mrs. Breckinridge could not have held back her message any more than you could keep the Middle Fork from flowing toward the Ohio.

The syllabus included a section titled "Getting Along with Supervisors" and described "happy relations, lack of self-consciousness under observation, readiness to accept criticism and willingness to profit by it." There was a series of thirty-two medical lectures on topics ranging from early pregnancy nutrition to technical complications such as "Rupture of the Uterus, Inversion of the Uterus." There were thirty-six classroom presentations, some with hands-on demonstrations on a mannequin. To demonstrate fetal development and abnormalities, the school used fifty-six preserved human specimens.

"I'm glad I've already been through nurses' training," Evelyn blurted out when she saw the first of the study fetuses floating in formaldehyde in its large glass jar. "But it's different when it's a tiny baby, don't you think?" Donna nodded silently. She felt the same uneasiness. That was a good thing about being in class with Evelyn. She usually expressed things no one else wanted to, and let the consequences sort themselves out.

To graduate, each nurse had to deliver a minimum of twenty normal maternity cases under the supervision of her instructor. These deliveries included five in the hospital and five out on district to prepare the nurse for conditions she would encounter in the rustic homes.

The nurses learned each step, beginning with registration – what they called "booking the case" – through the specific pre-natal exam procedures. The sequence began with nutritional recommendations and monthly checkups until the woman entered the final trimester. Then checkups were conducted every two weeks until the final month, when the woman was seen weekly in her home. Mothers-to-be came to their closest outpost clinic for more complete examinations at certain points in their pregnancies. Of course, delivery dates were a variable. But knowing the expectant mother, special concerns, and her household situation was part of Mrs. Breckinridge's philosophy of improving the health of families. This practice – modeled after the proven European approach – was the reason maternal and newborn mortality in the FNS service area was dropping below the national average.

"This, students, is your most valuable piece of medical equipment," Miss Gilbert said, slowly bringing from a set of saddlebags an Eveready flashlight. "Pack it carefully and always carry extra batteries." Heavy emphasis was placed on a nurse's ability to attend a birth in low light conditions, since there was no electricity in the area homes.

"You will *never* be without your copy of *Medical Routine.* By now you understand that you are practicing in special circumstances. This book will be your authority on what you may – and may not – do in emergency cases." Donna opened the compact, blue leatherette-covered book and fanned through its five hundred pages. She'd seen treatment for snake and lizard bites, mushroom poisoning, dog and other animal bites, and the more conventional medical concerns. Now it was time to memorize the section on midwifery. Miss Gilbert continued displaying the contents of the FNS delivery kit, which included different supplies than their standard nursing bags. Packed, it weighed forty-two pounds. "Think of this as a delivery room in a saddlebag," their teacher said. "It's all you will have on district. I don't need to tell you how critical it is to have it properly packed at all times. If you need it in a hurry, you're going to need everything in it!"

The FNS saddlebag had been perfected over the years since Mrs. Breckinridge first pioneered the technique in 1925. Clusters of related supplies were separated in color-coded cotton bags – five curved kidney-shaped basins that nested together, a rubber sheet, aprons, caps, masks, towel, a collection of essential supplies for both mother and baby. The left bag was full of medicines: Unguentine and Ichthammol salves; sulphur; enema supplies; pitocin; scissors and clamps for cutting the umbilical cord; mercurochrome for the newborn's eyes; and dozens of emergency supplies such as hypo syringes, Ergotrate, codeine sulfate, morphine sulfate, and brandy. The leather saddle bag had pouches beneath the flap for carrying fragile vials in an upright position. The right side contained a stethoscope, measuring tapes, test tubes and holders, scales, and baby care items. The weight of each side was evenly balanced so it would stay put behind the saddle.

Nurses set up for a delivery in a very specific order. "When not in too great a haste," the nurse midwife was to find something upon which to lay out her supplies and cover it with newspapers or clean paper napkins. If there wasn't a table, she was to use any level surface – a sewing machine cabinet, box, or chair. She'd first set up a canned-heat Sterno outfit with which to boil the Number One basin to sterilize tools: Cord ties, scissors, two clamps, obstetric suture, hypo syringe and two needles. She was to boil her rubber gloves, also. Then each basin was swabbed with Lysol to sanitize it.

The hypo was filled with Ergotrate and placed so the nurse could grasp it while her other hand was on the patient's abdomen.

Instruction number fourteen was: "Place, on table, in handy place, the bottle of Brandy."

When all the tools and supplies were sterilized and laid out, they were covered with another sheet of clean newspaper, while awaiting the baby's arrival. Plenty of water was boiled to decontaminate it for washing after the birth. A lard can was commonly used for a slop pail to contain soiled materials. A receiving blanket was to be warmed.

When the baby's head showed about six centimeters in diameter, the nurse would place two fingers on its head with each labor pain, to control its delivery. When the opening was adequate, the nurse would allow the baby's head to emerge between pains. Timing was critical at this point. Ideally, the head came before the next pain. The patient must pant, not push, to avoid tearing her perineum, which would lead to a lengthy and more painful recovery.

Immediately after the birth of the head, the nurse was to quickly wipe the baby's nose, mouth and eyes with a dry sponge, then she must feel with her trained fingers the orientation of the umbilical cord. If the cord was around the baby's neck, she hooked it with a finger, and slid it over the baby's head to keep the blood flow from getting interrupted. If the cord was too tight for this maneuver, the nurse was to clamp the cord in two places and cut between the clamps. "The entire time spent checking the cord and removing it should not be more than five to ten seconds," the manual instructed.

With that critical situation passed, the nurse waited for the rotation of the baby in order for the shoulders to emerge. Sometimes she had to assist this process. With the next pain, and not before, she applied a gentle downward and forward pull on the head, so that the forward shoulder was visible. Then she did an upward pull so that the second shoulder followed easily and slowly to avoid tearing. The rest of the baby's body followed naturally. She was to clear mucous from the throat, and hang the baby by its feet briefly if necessary. The legendary spank was not part of the FNS process. Once the pulse stopped in the umbilical cord, it was clamped in two places and cut between. If the baby was breathing normally, the nurse could tend the woman. If the baby needed care for asphyxia, the nurse attended it immediately, leaving mother's care for the moment. "At this stage, getting a live baby is more important than the possible harm of leaving the mother," the instructions stated.

Once the placenta appeared, meaning separation had occurred, the mother was encouraged to give another push to expel it. Incomplete separation, and tearing from the uterus results in hemorrhage, the most common cause of maternal death in childbirth, especially if the mother is anemic. Worn-down women were often anemic, in spite of the advice the nurses gave about diet. At this point, the prepared shot was given to reduce the likelihood of uncontrollable bleeding.

Mrs. Breckinridge entered the classroom. It was her custom to visit the school about once a week, and the six nurses always responded by straightening up in their hard oak chairs. She spent a few minutes listening to the instruction, and sometimes added a timely comment. "On your own," she began one day, "you may have observed an important characteristic of the families you will be serving. Unlike much of the world which has become intermixed, Kentucky people are homogenous American stock. Unions of mixed genetics can create consequences of concern to the birth process. Here you will not have the problem of a large Scandinavian head trying to begin life by passing through a petite Anglo pelvis."

In class one strenuous afternoon in July, Donna was near exhaustion but did not want to show it. She allowed her thoughts to detour from the lecture on "Opthalmia Neonatorum" and thought about the mountain home conditions . . . dark . . . no running water, and what you bring indoors is cold and full of contagion. Sometimes no window glass so the weather blows right through . . . flies in hot weather, snakes living under the gaping floor boards . . . she thought about the families she'd seen. It was easy to spot the effects of poor nutrition, poor dental health, intestinal parasites, and large families sharing in the meager yields of their milk cows, chickens and gardens. She recalled Mrs. Breckinridge's phrase, "the load of drudgery, labor and responsibility called for in your task at hand . . ." She thought about the tomato and watermelon seeds that Myra had sent her. Donna had decided to plant them in the Wendover garden, even though it meant she could only tend them on her outings there. She was beginning to wonder if she'd last long enough in Kentucky to see them through to harvest. But then, there was the tomato-tasting contest she and Ellery had agreed on back in February. She wondered if he even remembered it.

Her thoughts were interrupted when Mrs. Breckinridge entered the classroom.

It seemed to Donna that the woman expected super-human performance from her staff. Evelyn had not long ago expressed her exasperation. "That Mrs. Breckinridge always gets a little more out of us than we have to give," she declared.

It was true. The founder was known for her unbending standards and lofty expectations. But she also had a knack for sensing when a person was mentally spent, or in emotional trouble. She sat quietly through the rest of the lesson, and before the students were released she stood, straightened her jacket and looked them over, her eyes sincere and maternal. For a short woman, she had mighty presence. They could tell she had something to say.

"My dears, by now you have discovered that you are being asked to do the near-impossible," she began. "Simply put, it is because we believe you *can* do it. Since our beginnings, your colleagues have attended over six thousand births, three-fourths of them in the home. We have proven that our techniques are as safe as a city hospital. Our maternal death rate is a fraction of what it is in the rest of the nation."

She had a way of bolstering your morale. "My dears, you are taking part in the making of history."

⌒ ⌒

After dinner, Donna switched on the pin-up lamp over her desk and while studying by some of the only electric lights in the county, her courage returned. She was comforted knowing that at first she'd be paired with an experienced nurse-midwife, so she alone wouldn't have to provide the three – sometimes four – hands even a normal delivery called for; not to mention one of those complicated situations; and the nearest doctor hours away.

She took out clean paper and wrote home:

> *Dearest ones,*
> *My midwife schooling is going hard, but I am determined to make it. We need midwives; even though some men are away in the war, women are still having babies, and a dozen of our staff went home to England.*
> *Today we manipulated a fetus doll through a pelvis model, to get real practice if there is a difficult presentation. Did I say they turned out the lights so we had to feel the process in the dark? My hands aren't as slender as some of the students, so it took me longer to manage some of the movements. But after some practice my times were good. We practiced suturing on some butchered pigs' feet they brought in for us. We made a contest out of it – who could do the smallest stitch. You can guess mine didn't win any prizes, but when the time comes, my stitches will sure hold! Just another day in baby-catching school!*
> *I will sign off now to get some rest. Who can imagine what we'll do next! At least we won't have Scandinavian heads coming through Kentucky pelvises!*
> *That's what Mrs. B told us.*
> *Love, D*

Angels Come From Rockhouse Creek

"You not only knew your patient very well,
but you and God knew each other quite well, too.
After [the birth] was all over, [the mother] said,
'I knew you were scared. But I also knew you'd do it.'
And that sort of faith does something to you."

— Grace Reeder, former FNS nurse; FNS Oral History Project, 1979

*D*onna and Evelyn were proud they could add C.M. to their names now. They'd passed their examinations and graduated from the Frontier Graduate School of Nursing. Donna received a letter from Mrs. Breckinridge announcing the date that she passed her state exams and that she was certified by the state to practice midwifery. Her letter concluded:

> *I am proud to have you as one of the graduates of the school.*
> *With highest personal regards, and every good wish for you in the future years.*
>
> > *I am yours sincerely,*
> > *Mary Breckinridge*

The letter made Donna proud and as she sat in her dorm room reading it again, Evelyn entered, her letter in her hand.

"She sure sent a nice letter," Donna said, not wanting to brag about the special message Mrs. Breckinridge had written to her.

"It's probably the same letter for everyone who passes," Evelyn said, holding hers out for Donna to see. "They need us right now. She's trying to keep us happy."

Feeling a little like Evelyn had trespassed on something personal, Donna put her letter in a safe place where she could take it out and read it again later. "Well, I need the FNS as much as they need me," Donna said. "I have no intention of going back to the hospital in Petoskey where a nurse can go a whole week without feeling like she's helped a real human."

Donna mailed her diploma home to Myra for safekeeping. Donna wasn't the type to brag, but if her aunt put the document in a frame and hung it near the Biblical quote in the dining room, everyone would see it there, announcing Donna's achievement in a quiet kind of way.

Without any delay for pomp and circumstance, the young women were put to work at the Hyden Hospital until each would be assigned to an outpost to work alongside a more experienced nurse-midwife for a time. Donna resumed nursing tasks again, pleased with the demands of the job. She looked forward to her new purpose here in Appalachian Kentucky. Six months of classroom and intense studies were behind her. She knew she'd be called at irregular hours and would work long days, but it was a cadence she was accustomed to.

"You'uns are all invited to a potluck social tomorrow night," Lettie, one of the FNS housekeepers, announced to the women. "if you c'n get away, it's up to our school. My family will be there, and you'uns c'n set with us. Thar's s'posed to be singin' but I don't know what else."

Country folks love their potluck dinners and they are important social events. Donna and her nurse friends thought it would be a good way to get better acquainted in an off-duty way, and they prepared two special dishes to share. They boiled wheat noodles and made a casserole of canned tuna from the store. For a dessert, they made white-bread pudding with cinnamon and raisins. It was too far to walk, so they rode down the Thousandsticks hill, followed Rockhouse Creek, and made their way up to the little schoolhouse. They spotted Lettie and joined her family group. The spread of foods included sweet-potato pie, ham and potatoes, stewed tomatoes and biscuits. The evening took a turn away from a neighborhood gathering when a half-dozen unfamiliar missionaries stood and introduced themselves.

When everyone was finishing their meal, the missionaries passed around shapenote songbooks. A folding pump organ emerged from a battered-looking wooden case, a man sat in front of it, pumped out wheezing tones with his feet and hands, and the singing began. After a few songs, the leader, a gaunt man with a wreath of gray hair, stood and with his arms outstretched, silenced the group. He asked them to join him in prayer, closing his eyes. He began kindly enough, sending thanks for the bounties they shared; then he pitched a fire and brimstone story, using the inertia of fear to herd the people's thinking his way. When it seemed he was closing out his prayer, his voice quavered and rose in pitch as he made a fervent plea for God to "forgive the atheists on the hill." Donna raised her bowed head to see his bony hands shaking in a "woe-is-me" gesture. There could be no other meaning than the people at the Hyden hospital atop Thousandsticks. He went on to say something about gates being open for those who repent – who are seen in a special light by the Lord.

"This here's turned out to be a real hard-shell preacher," Lettie said to the nurses. "Some people get riled when they're told that even the least-ones are lost to damnation. Them holiness folks say that unless a baby has witnessed, the little dearies burn in hell along with the big old experienced sinners."

This shift in the festivities sounded an alarm in Donna, because the stranger had implicated the hardworking people she worked closely with – doctors, nurses, midwives, secretaries, cooks, housekeepers, and even Ellery the caring horseshoer and the handymen who kept the hospital open to serve all comers day and night. Why did they need any "forgiveness?" If any of these pious strangers needed help, the hospital staff would tend them without question, without judgment. There were no gates on the hospital at Hyden.

Was the old fellow aware that she and her harried colleagues had no time for anything but catching up on paperwork and reading the latest nursing bulletins on Sundays? And some Sundays they were out on emergency calls. Did he judge them as lesser humans because they did not worship in his way? Was he using them to exalt himself?

Lettie interrupted Donna's runaway thoughts. "I hope they left their snakes at home!" She whispered in a loud, raspy voice in the general direction of the nurses. "Sometimes they pull a snake from outten a box, and after they wind up good in prayer, they let 'em crawl all over to prove they can hold off wickedness."

"If this is religion, give me none of it," Donna thought. It looked like a few of the potluck folks' minds were turned toward his philosophy. Donna asked Lettie if she felt that way.

"You got to know that these holiness folks aren't natured to you brought-on people with yer bottled medicines," she said. "They don't hold with needles and yer kind o' healin'. "To them, the old granny midwife was all they needed. They know their yarbs and poultices, which have done them just fine."

This was not a new revelation to Donna. She knew that medical attention was not welcomed by all. Some folks still insisted that grinding up a sulfur-smelling plant called devil's dung and putting it in a cloth bag around the neck stopped contagious diseases like tuberculosis. They carried a buckeye chestnut in their pocket to keep rheumatism away. She recalled Mrs. Breckinridge's wise words about modern treatments; "It's hard to believe in the invisible." Placing an axe under the bed was a tangible thing you could do and see. For generations the outcome of folk remedies like that had been favorable enough that families sprouted six to eight live children. But the tally of lost children and women appeared in the form of grave markers on the hills above the homes.

"I hope for the children's sake, we can overcome their superstitions," Donna said to Lettie.

The evening's activities came to a close and the nurses rode back up to their quarters at the hospital compound.

Donna was still troubled by the old preacher's message. She had never thought about her colleagues' religious leanings. They rarely had time to think of going to any of the few churches in the area. They were dedicated to giving their skills, knowledge, time and medical training to whoever needed it, which seemed worthy of favorable judgment. Yes, she concluded, everyone I work with is a Good Samaritan. No doubt about it. We've chosen this place over others with comforts, conveniences and a healthy salary. And we grieve just like everyone else when someone is lost to illness or injury.

She recalled the words on the faded plaque above the door in their dining room at home:

"Bear ye one another's burdens and so fulfill the law of Christ. – Galatians, 6:2"

Those simple words of Apostle Paul were pretty much the core of the Carroll family values, and were reinforced again and again during her work here in Kentucky. She knew the shank-spindled old preacher and his "holiness folks" meant no harm, but Donna just chalked it up to a bit of ignorance to the greater meaning.

A late night call came in for the midwife.

"My woman's punishin' hard," the man said. Donna and the senior nurse, Rosie, saddled up. Slinging her delivery bags over her saddle, Rosie said to the man, "We can make better time without having to wait for you to come along on your mule." She found her way to the creek by sound, Donna following behind on Jefferson. Bucky, not to be left behind, fell in behind the horse.

Donna knew the way up the creek in the daytime. It seemed a lot rockier and steeper in the dark. No matter the weather, terrain or conditions, the Frontier Nurse philosophy was, "If the father can come to us, we can go to the mother." In the pitch dark, with no sense of the horizon, the motion gave Donna vertigo. She had to fight the unsettling feeling of losing her balance. She discovered it helped if she put equal pressure on each stirrup and just let Jefferson make his way. Branches slapped her in the face as she rode through the blackness. She couldn't worry about her dog – if he became separated, he knew the way back to the center.

The woman was in the transitional stage of labor when they arrived. This was her fourth birth. Two of her children had gone to a neighbor's for the night. Her oldest, a nine-year-old boy, stayed at the home in case his help was called for – running for a neighbor, cleaning a lamp, tending the wood stove. He had a basin of boiling water all ready. The nurses prepared as well as they could in spite of the urgency. They wiped basins with Lysol and put on their aprons and gloves. There wasn't much of a wait before the baby's head emerged. As Donna wiped its nose, mouth and eyes, she heard the father hurry into the cabin. The cord was around the baby's neck, cutting off its circulation. While Rosie coached the mother on when to push and when to pant, Donna deftly reached in, slipped the cord over the baby's head, and checked for other loops.

She held any comment about the troubling condition of the baby, who was an unhealthy color.

Donna's mind raced. "We cannot work delivering babies and in any way be atheists. We do our best to bring a healthy baby into the world, but we are a small part of the process." Rosie gave the shot of Ergotrate.

The baby drew in a large breath and cried out, gaining good color.

"You have a new baby girl! Pink is such a lovely color," Donna said, directing the double-meaning to Rosie. But after delivering the placenta, the woman gushed blood – the much-feared hemorrhage. The nurses gave each other a silent knowing look, and began emergency treatment in their steady manner. Sensing the situation, the father and boy began praying.

Phrases from her recent training went through Donna's mind. She recalled Mrs. Breckinridge standing in front of the classroom, telling the nurses to demonstrate confidence to the patient. "You will not let them down," she'd said.

"We thought they was more time, or I'da' got a sooner start to fetch you," the man apologized. "I am good-pleased you were here in our time of need."

"We do like to have a little more time to prepare, but your wife has done well so far," Donna said, mustering all the confidence she could in her voice. She sent the boy outside for smooth stones to heat in the coals. While Rosie tended the mother, the father and Donna propped the foot of the bed up on a pair of firewood chunks. Donna rolled up towels to heat near the fire, asking the father to keep turning them. She also asked him to round up canning jars and fill them with hot water to keep the woman warm. This was critical to keep her from going into shock, or the vital organs could cease to function. The nurses gave rectal saline to replace her fluids, and it seemed like hours, but the bleeding stopped before the woman lost more than about a pint of blood. They kept her warm by rotating the heated towels, stones and canning jars. Both nurses stayed until the danger had lessened, then made plans to "special" her, meaning they would take turns 'round-the clock, attending her for several more days. Thanks to the FNS saddlebag technique, the mother would recover.

Satisfied that they'd decided what was needed, Donna prepared to leave. The little boy, clutching her shirtsleeve, looked up at her. "I do believe angels come from Rockhouse Creek," he said, referring to their hospital above the creek at Hyden.

Donna never thought of herself as an angel, but as long as she didn't let it go to her head, it was okay.

Mistook fer a 'Possum

"Papa got hisself shot!" gushed the little boy, nearly breathless after his four-mile run to the Confluence outpost. "And the hurt's goin' hard on him!"

"Saddle up Jefferson while I prepare my kit please, Julia," Donna ordered the young courier in her steady voice. The child was wet up to his crotch, having crossed the Brushy Fork, and he must have barked his shin. A bloodstain blurred into the denim below the patched knee of his overalls. "You're Robbie, and your family name is Mackey, is that right, young man?"

"Yes'm. We're above the Brushy Fork a piece."

"I know the place. I'll leave directly." Turning to Julia, she added in her kind but authoritative tone, "Check the boy's leg and see that he dries out before he heads back home." With a wink at the boy she added, "I bet we've got some warm serviceberry cobbler to feed this little feller, soon as he catches his breath. The stove could use some new company for a time."

Within minutes, Donna was lashing her saddlebags on her horse. As always, she seemed to cheat gravity as she planted her left boot into the near side stirrup, and swung her stocky body into the saddle to a series of familiar leather squeaks.

Instead of heading away at a gallop as her eager spirit may have wished, Donna urged the horse into a fast walk. She had learned early in her trail experience with the FNS that an unhurried, steady go was the fastest way to get to people in need of medical attention in these steep, rugged woods. Bucky, as usual, trotted along in front, only pausing when they came to any kind of choice in the trail.

A Tennessee Walking horse like Jefferson can average about six miles an hour. Adding in time for the bad parts of the trail, Donna could fairly well guess when she would arrive, and the likely condition of the boy's father. The bleeding would have stopped. She might have to locate the lead bullet and keep the man calm while she removed it. Then there was the possibility of blood poisoning, a condition as threatening as the bullet wound.

Donna would not ask about the cause of the incident. "Why" was not a nurse's business. Mrs. Breckinridge made this very clear to each nurse. "When someone is shot and we are called, our business is nursing. We do all we can. The fight behind it is not our concern." Donna had been trained to treat and heal; not to judge. But for some of the nurses this lesson was harder to master than a hands-on skill like suturing a ragged wound or bringing down a fever. Evelyn, for one, buzzed about gunshot injuries and came up with entertaining explanations, which always made Donna uncomfortable.

By the time Donna joined the FNS, most of the Kentucky people were agreeable to the brought-on nurses' way of keeping complete records on each person. But the FNS goal of registering every family in their service area had not been achieved, and it was looking as though it may never be. There were still unknown families. These were the most superstitious, or families that held dogmatically to beliefs that were at odds with medicine. The most reclusive ones kept their names from being written anywhere, even in the compassionate nurses' confidential records. No doubt these families had their sickness, mismanaged births, their burns, lesions and accidents, but they preferred to stay out of the realm of the FNS. There was little to do but abide their ways. These places loomed mysterious and unknown as the nurses passed them by on their rounds.

As Jefferson made his way through the hardwoods, Donna wondered if this injury was the result of a family feud of long-forgotten origin; or if the gunshot would be explained away with the common fable that the hapless victim had been "mistook fer a possum." Movement in the underbrush could mean a four-footed main dish, so naturally, a shot would be fired. In unspoken truth, some grazings were committed by shadowy locals who operated liquor stills. There were a few of these covert operations scattered around the woods and the owners lived in perennial fear of the Revenuers snooping around too close. Constant vigilance made these moonshiners flinchy. Sudden movement in the brush near their outbuilding would trigger a warning shot. None of these

characters wanted to kill anyone – that would be a serious federal crime. Instead, a little hazing back with a squirrel rifle usually
solved the problem of a pesky government snoop hanging around
– for awhile, anyway.

Donna had no hankering for liquor, so it was hard for her to
understand that kind of protective zeal. She puzzled what would
cause people to defend their crude hissing stills to that length.

"There you go, judging again," she scolded herself out loud.
"How this guy got shot is of no matter." She reminded herself
of Mrs. Breckinridge, who had ministered to illness and injury
enough for a dozen lifetimes. The woman, even if a little intimi-
dating, was a fine mentor with the philosophy that everyone deserved the best treatment possible, free of judgment.

Jefferson's nodding sneeze brought Donna's thoughts back to
the brushy trail, and the conditions she was likely to face in the
remote home of the injured man. Would there be a vicious dog?
Enough light? Clean water?

She approached the little settlement – a clearing in the hem-
lock and ash trees, a cabin, some ramshackle pig fencing and a
chicken coop. She dismounted and removed her kit from the saddlebag, scattering chickens as she approached the house. Maude,
in a homemade dress, anklets and sad-looking oxfords, motioned
her into the dark room beyond the kitchen where her husband
lay, pale and stoic. The smell of metabolizing liquor hung in the
room. This was probably the only "medicine" they had, and if it
served to keep the man calm, Donna could accept that.

The nurse cleaned up the fellow's bloody leg for a close look.
The bullet had exited, leaving a jagged tear in his lower leg, but it
had missed bone and tendons. The wound was not life-threaten-
ing. Prompt cleansing, some stitches, and proper on-going care
was critical. Donna sterilized her tools and began.

After treating the man, Donna put her things back in her bag
and stepped back in to the main room. The woman followed.
Donna instructed her to keep his leg elevated to help in the healing. "Send word as fast as you can, the first sign of fever. If it doesn't
heal right, he could lose his leg." The woman was very attentive.
Losing the man of the house would have serious consequences in
the hard-scrabble life of rural Kentucky. Chopping wood, killing

game and keeping the place in repair would all fall to her and her children, adding a huge burden to their already-hard life.

And a crippled man was an unthinkable burden, almost worse than dead, if you really thought it out.

Mountain Justice,
In and Beyond the Courtroom

"My daddy's a good citizen. He packs a gun, an' has kilt two men, an' he takes his dram, but he hain't never stole even a chicken."

— quote in *Wide Neighborhoods*

"You goin' to the Gladwell shootin' trial?" was the talk around town. It was impossible to ignore. Evelyn asked Lettie, the Hyden housekeeper, what she felt about the killing of Cecil Gladwell, and the two men accused of the crime.

"Well . . ." she drawled, "thar's shootin' . . . thar's killin' . . . and thar's murder." She paused. "And it seems like this one started out as a shootin' but things went all wrong. It turned into a killin' and now they's treatin' it more like murder."

Evelyn had learned that Lettie was related to the accused men as well as the victim. But it surprised her when Lettie explained, "O' course most the town is related to one side or t'other. And the affray left Cecil's widow and young'uns which is gonna ire up the rest o' the folks who's not kin." The housekeeper shook her head. "It's gonna be a nervous time in town all the while that trial's goin' on."

This was the kind of event that thrilled Evelyn.

"When yer related to people on both sides, yer torn right down the middle," Lettie told her.

"Mrs. Breckinridge doesn't want any of us getting involved with things like this." Donna knew she'd be ignored, but reminded Evelyn anyway. "We're to stay ignorant so we can treat everyone the same."

But the tragedy intrigued Evelyn. Nothing like this ever happened in her hometown. Everyone was so . . . *sophisticated* there. The courthouse in her hometown kept busy renewing auto licenses and holding justice court for petty civil disputes.

Elwood Roberts and Arnold Wadsworth were to go on trial for the shooting death of Cecil Gladwell. The fatal affray began on a warm, spring Saturday evening in the town pool hall and moved outside into the muddy street. There was some confused scuffling, and shots split the evening air, leaving one man dead and one with powder burns on his arm. The newspaper reported that the dead man was shot through the heart. Local men scoffed that at such close range, a shot through the heart didn't really count for much.

There were bystanders, but only one who could have clearly seen Cecil's right arm and hand, which he would have used to fire his gun. Immediately afterwards, Kilmer, the one witness, said that Cecil was looking right at Arnold. "I see'd him pull his gun," he said. "Then I heer'd shots, and there was Cecil, dead as a hammer."

Like Lettie said, the dead man's roots were tangled with nearly everyone's family tree in town. The idea that Cecil might have been at fault was not a popular notion. The biggest rumble became whether or not the dead man had pulled a gun and fired first, which would lead to a less ominous outcome for the defendants, possibly exonerating them from the murder charge. But someone had to suffer for the murderous attack on Cecil.

People speculated that the problem began over a long-ago raid on a still. The family had always suspected a neighbor who informed on people for the reward money that revenuers paid for tips. Others thought it was because the deceased was married to the sister of one of the accused men. There may have been a disrespectful incident that triggered retaliation. For whatever reason, the man was dead and somebody had to pay. Strong feelings bubbled close to the surface and the townsfolk were separating like fire and ice. The bulk of sympathy rested on the side of the victim.

Having lived among the Kentucky people for a short while, Donna had begun to understand their ethical pinnings and values. Mountain men lost no social status for killing someone the likes of a traitorous neighbor or a cheating, horse-abusing bootlegger. If a man was caught stealing, it was regarded as a much more serious crime.

Mrs. Breckinridge had told the nurses that "in spite of the Kentucky mountain man's reputation, they are chivalrous to women. You may go out alone on your calls day or night, and you will be safe around them. Our young female couriers may feel completely safe with one as an escort through the woods." She paused, looking around the table at each nurse, and raised an index finger to emphasize her point. "In return for this courtesy and protection, we are to remain neutral. We hear nothing; we see nothing, nor do we say anything regarding their business. Of course, when you approach their neighborhoods, for you to be safe, they must recognize you first. So always wear your uniform. And it's a good idea to keep up a steady conversation with your horse or your dog."

Everyone knew Roberts and Wadsworth could not get a fair trial in Hyden with a jury of Leslie County people. The summons went out in neighboring Knott County for "non-related, intelligent, sober, discreet citizens and housewives to appear at nine o'clock in the morning to try the case in the Leslie Circuit Court in Hyden."

Seventy-five prospective jurors were summoned. Jury selection was hasty, the prosecuting attorney carrying out his part as casually as if this was nothing more consequential than a Sunday picnic. The defendants were jailed in another county. The court requested extra peace-keeping reinforcements and state police escorted the defendants to the trial.

The courtroom was packed as the trial began. Many of the defense lawyer's objections were overruled. The judge acted like he was late for tee time at the country club.

People shifted in their creaky chairs, but they sat all day, watching patiently as the bailiff brought water and food to the judge, and cleared away the dirty plates. No one recognized the young woman who slipped into the back row with a scarf over her dark curls as one of the Hyden nurses. The defense lawyer was not able to produce Kilmer, the witness who had actually seen Cecil's movements right before the shots were fired. The man had skipped out.

Without a strong defense witness, the lawyer had to find a new angle. He paused while delivering his summation. He wiped his forehead again. Looking each of the twelve jurors in the eye, he began to persuade them that it was unjust to condemn two men when it only requires one man to fire a lethal shot. "Who among you," he asked, "could send either man to prison for life for willful murder when there was no way to prove who fired the fatal shot?" He did everything he could to dislodge the prosecutor's case with the jury.

The verdict came back: Guilty of voluntary manslaughter. The sentence: Two years in the Kentucky State Reformatory at La Grange. As Evelyn left the courthouse, she heard someone say, "Two years ain't long enough fer folks to ferget. I'll bound they'll be made to pay more dearly. They may not even make it home from the pen."

It was late when Evelyn returned to the Hyden compound, confessing that after her clinic duties she had spent her afternoon at the courthouse. "Oh, it was so exciting!" she reported. "The two men on trial seemed so harmless. They didn't look like the killing type. The younger one seemed so honorable, always saying 'yes sir' and 'if you please.' He looked so young."

The nurses gathered around the table and asked for more detail. "Their defense lawyer kept getting overruled," Evelyn told them. "His key witness never showed up. You could tell he was struggling. The judge wasn't lenient. He just kept saying it would be up to the jury to decide. The talk was that the witness, a man named Kilmer, was scared of testifying in front of all Cecil's kin. I heard someone say, 'If'n he said anything against Cecil, and those two get off easy, Kilmer would be another one sufferin' the pain.' Can you blame him for skipping?" she asked rhetorically.

The nurses agreed it was a tough spot for him to be in.

"Seeing those two being led off to prison was just awful." She continued. "I just wanted to wind the clock back to that evening in the pool hall and march through the whole bunch of 'em and take away all their guns. No one would be in this fix. When it was all over, there was a feeling in the air that the issue was not really settled for good, and I guess that's where we come in when we get those emergency calls."

Agreeing, the women scooted their chairs from the table, said good night and shuffled off to their dorm rooms.

Donna was working at the Beech Fork nursing center one Saturday evening when the senior nurse left for her weekend off. In stocking feet and her favorite old pullover sweater, she was looking forward to catching up on letters and reading. A courier had come from Wendover to pick up the week's records. Rather than ride back that evening, she was staying in the guest bedroom. The two women had just finished dinner when a boy's voice called from outside. "Mommy's havin' fits," said the frightened boy. "She cain't lie still. It skeert Daddy, but he couldn't make the trip hisself." His father sent the boy on their mule to get a nurse's help.

The woman was a registered pre-natal. Fearing the seizures that can develop with toxemia, Donna quickly checked the woman's file but saw no record of high blood pressure or protein in her urine tests.

The courier asked if Donna wanted some help holding a lantern for the dark ride up and back.

"I sure wouldn't turn it down," Donna said gratefully, and turned to the boy.

"Young man, please saddle our horses while we get ready. We'll go on ahead to make the best time we can. You come along on your mule and Bucky can follow you if you'd like his company."

It was more than four miles to the house, and before long darkness was upon them. The area was known for feuding but Donna could not refuse to help any of their registered patients. There were long stretches of lonely woods with no friendly lamp light or neighborliness. She missed the company and reassurance of the senior nurse. The courier's lantern didn't do much more than shine a circle a few feet ahead of them, but the light helped announce their presence. Donna's ears strained to compensate for the blackness of the night. The crickets had stopped chirping. The women revived their chatter, as Mrs. Breckinridge had suggested, and to dilute their anxiety. Donna noticed a faint reflection on what could only be a gun barrel, but did not say anything to the courier. There's no reason to alarm the girl if she hasn't noticed, Donna thought. No one is going to shoot us, she reassured herself.

By now, Donna was comfortable that people kept a protective watch for the FNS nurses, but it was too dark for anyone to recognize her uniform. Approaching hoof steps could trigger a warning shot or worse. On this outing it was probably a good thing that Bucky wasn't running ahead in his usual way. He may have alarmed one of these rifle-toting mountain men and met a terrible fate. This time it was Jefferson who telegraphed something unusual. Donna knew they were getting near the house. The horse shuddered and stopped abruptly. Donna nudged him along, reining him one way then the other to get him to continue. He took a few unsteady steps, then lunged, nearly leaving Donna behind. Somehow she stayed on. Stroking his neck she said, "Easy boy . . . settle down now. Just a little farther." He resumed his steady walk up to the fence. "Must have been a snake on the path," Donna thought.

She hollered to the family. A man's muffled voice told her to come in. As she began setting up to tend the woman, she noticed a man sitting in the shadows with an obvious head injury. The mother's blood pressure was elevated. She was not well, but evidently her "fits" were over. Donna told the woman she should have someone bring her to the hospital if she worsened. Then she approached the man and asked if she could tend his injury. His hair was bloody and matted. A black, grim-looking streak of dried blood ran down the side of his head.

"No, ma'am, I need to leave it just as it is until the sheriff has a chance to see what happened," he said, "even if it takes till Tuesday."

Donna knew better than to press him further for an explanation. She assured him that if he needed medical help, he could seek it from her safely and privately. Donna and the courier stayed long enough to see that the pregnant woman settled down. The man sat there in the dark the entire time. Knowing the sheriff had been summoned was little comfort. Who knew what could happen in the meantime? It hadn't been that long ago that federal agents had carelessly shot into a home near Beech Fork, thinking it was a moonshine operation. They killed the man and his wife in front of their two tiny children.

On their way back down the dark trail, Donna discussed the likely cause of the woman's distress. It was obvious that her problems were emotional, not physical.

"That's a poor time to find yourself in the middle of a feud," Donna said. "I firmly believe an unborn baby can sense trouble going on around its mother, especially at her stage. I'll mark the fracas on her chart so we'll keep it in mind as we progress through her pre-natals."

The sheriff did show up later, they learned, and the next day the hills were full of rumors. The fact was that one man had been shot to death. The sheriff found the body alongside the trail near the home. Donna realized that Jefferson had probably smelled the man's blood, which was what spooked the horse.

The nurses knew the man who had been killed. He was from a respected family, and had a nice wife and three children. Either he was doing something that threatened someone, or he was simply in the wrong place at the wrong time. "The 'why' is of no matter now," Donna thought. "It's a shame a grudge can make its evil way into a baby's world when they're so innocent."

After that night's excitement, Donna pondered the mountain people and their unusual emergency calls. She was still troubled about the killing and wrote home to take her mind off it. She began:

> *Dearest ones,*
>
> *I'm at Beech Fork center alone this weekend. Marian, the senior nurse, is off on a much-needed weekend, so I'm holding it down myself. Of course I have Bucky indoors with me. He is a good companion.*
>
> *I made an emergency call on a pre-natal. Julia, one of the couriers, rode up there with me. It was dark, but the horses know the way.*
>
> *It's good to meet more of the people. They are independent and quiet. They don't ask for much. Sure they have their squabbles, but don't we all?*
>
> *When it comes to the newborns, you could not find more caring people. They cherish the little ones no matter how many they already have to care for. But somewhere along a little boy's path to growing up, tender care is laid aside. Boys turn tough-edged like sugar that's left to boil too long. Young men start carrying loaded guns, eager to defend their honor, property, women, stills or sometimes just rumors of such.*
>
> *The men treat us nurses properly and even protect us, but woe to the fellow who ventures somewhere he doesn't belong. This week's newspaper reported that a man was sentenced to one year in the state pen for child desertion; there was a two-year sentence for a killing, and a drunk man got fined $10 for shooting out a window.*

But in these mountains, some crimes never reach the paper. Woods trials, conviction and punishment are carried out far away from any courthouse.

It seems that actions – or misactions – are never forgiven or forgotten. We treat gunshots from revenge shootings, grudge shootings and moonshine shootings. Sometimes it's too late. Sometimes it leaves a widow and children.

And the circle goes on. These children grow up, get guns, get mad, get even . . .

Donna stopped and turned out her lamp. In the morning she slipped the letter in her journal and never mailed it.

Bean-Stringing, Bartering, Workings and Stir-Offs

"There wasn't very much money to be got a hold of."

— Della Gay, FNS Oral History Project, 1979

"*I*f you can't think of a thing more for me to do, Miss Evelyn, I think I'll leave out directly," said Jennie, the housekeeper at the Brutus outpost. "We're havin' a bean-stringin' and folks will be happenin' in anytime."

"A bean-stringing! Now doesn't that sound quaint," Evelyn said. "Do you mind if I come along?" She joined Jennie and they walked together the short way up Bullskin Creek to the girl's home.

Back at the outpost she reported on her evening, "They cooperate so nicely!" Evelyn began. "Of course there's some gossip, but it was mostly friendly. They each bring in their bushels of beans and sit in a circle. They snap the ends off and throw them in a tub. Then some women take a long needle and thread, and run every single bean pod through a certain way so they'll hang in a bunch and won't mold. They hang the bunches up on nails in their rafters. That way they have beans all winter. When they want some for a meal, they soak one of the bunches overnight, and simmer it with bacon or a piece of ham."

"It sounds delicious. I can almost smell it," the other nurse interrupted. Evelyn went on. "The men were outside butchering hogs, and I went out but I couldn't watch it for long, so I stayed in with the women. You know, as revolting as butchering is, I'd rather count on a Kentucky boy for survival than any one of those highbrow boys back home. City boys can hurt themselves closing a jackknife! They think ham comes from a factory!"

Nurse working over step stove; shucky beans hanging from rafters – *FNS photo, courtesy of Univ. of Kentucky archives.*

This was not exactly the land of plenty. There was precious little land that was farmable. Cash crops need acres of sun-bathed land to thrive, and a passable way to get to market, not beaten to a pulp on rough trails. In this shadowy land the only crops that succeeded had to be as tough and enduring as the people. The hills had been logged off so that the ground couldn't hold the rainwater as in the past. Unfettered runoff raced down the creek beds and created "tides" in the Middle Fork. The level tracts along the river flooded nearly every spring, sending precious seedlings and soils downstream forever. Crops had to be planted on higher patches of land, which ran up the hills to where it was too steep to hold soil or seed.

"Workin' the side hill crops is a lot easier on you if one leg is shorter'n the other'n," people joked. Corn, beans, potatoes and other root vegetables were the hardiest and most dependable – unless the hog got into the garden and grubbed it out. "Good burley" tobacco did well in the summer heat, but there weren't enough roads to make a commercial crop marketable. In an attempt to strangle the monster Depression, Franklin D. Roosevelt's Works Progress Administration put laborers to work. They built some roads in the Cumberland Plateau, but they only reached the larger towns. Few roads were carved into this country, but by 1941 Hazard was finally connected to Hyden. You could drive to Lexington by way of Manchester and London, but the farms weren't connected to the main roads.

In every direction, embankments and gullies revealed seams of rich, dark coal. The nation's industries were crying out for the fuel, but because roads and railroads didn't yet reach into the hollows, the "black gold" was landlocked. Folks dug at it and brought buckets of it home to fuel their stoves, but the vast bulk of the mineral had to remain where it had for millions of years.

The American chestnut tree had long been a forest staple. Once you freed the hearty nut from its prickly outer shell, it was delicious boiled like a beet, roasted like a potato, or dried. Children took chestnuts the size of chicken eggs to school for their lunch. Hogs were turned loose in the forests for its food source, and wild game was nourished by chestnuts. But in 1909 the prized trees began dying off when a deadly Asian tree fungus arrived in New York. All the way to Louisiana, the tallest trees in the forest sickened and died. By the 1940s, the epidemic had killed billions of the trees, wiping out a rich source of protein and valuable wood. It was a hard-hitting double loss for Kentucky's mountain people.

Electricity would not reach the area until 1948. Without transportation to markets there was no industry which meant no jobs. People survived on what they could milk from their cows, dig from the ground, hunt or cut from the woods, or carve from the bones of their poultry and livestock. They emptied the last grain from cloth feed sacks, and sewed their cotton prints into dresses. Women hoarded fabric scraps until there were enough to patch together a quilt. They coveted fabric sample books because they could pull the colorful squares off the pages to add to their quilt squares. Surpluses of any commodity were traded with neighbors. They carried on the pioneer tradition of barter and mutual workings to benefit one another.

The post office was the social center, where people gathered to share gossip and listen as someone read the newspaper headlines. If they learned a neighbor was laid up with a broken leg or illness, they turned out for a working to hoe his garden or bring in his bean crop. The cooperative labor went well beyond farm chores. Men would gather for a working to dig a well, peel logs and raise rafters, hew siding for a home, or roof a building in a day. They worked against the weather to get a house suitable for living before the season changed unfavorably.

"We, in the mountains, all of us, have the same social status," Mrs. Breckinridge said one evening at dinner, "whether we live in large houses on good bottom land, or in cabins on the remoter creeks. We help one another, and work for one another."

Schools operated on a schedule decided by local circumstances. Generally, school commenced in July after "fodderin' time," when the harvest and animal feed had been brought in. When the creeks started freezing, making it difficult for the children to get to school, sometime in January, school would be suspended. While in session, the school would host a play or pie supper. Women baked their best pies or made box lunches, and the community would gather at the one- or two-room frame and clapboard schoolhouses. Their homemaking would be auctioned off to raise money for pencils, paper and books for the students.

Nothing was thrown away if there was any hint of utility in it. "Goods boxes" were kept for lambing time, to place a bum lamb in. A clever father could add rockers to one to make a fine baby cradle. Barrels were made into heating stoves, with stovepipe cut from lard cans.

When Donna and Evelyn arrived in Kentucky, the FNS fee was up to two dollars per year per family and five dollars for the delivery of a baby. If a family couldn't scrape up the cash, they could pay in firewood, eggs, furs, potatoes, or a day's labor.

One afternoon, sipping a glass of sherry at Wendover, Mrs. Breckinridge recalled the time a boy brought a pair of guinea hens as payment for a delivery. "I'll never forget what he said as he was leaving, she recounted for the nurses, "'I aim to bring more till the baby's all paid for.'" Glancing at Lucile Hodges, the bookkeeper, she added, "The extra bookkeeping is well worth it, as long as the family retains its dignity." Lucile cast an eye-rolling glance at the others.

People also paid the Service with what they could make with their own hands. Straight-backed, cane-bottom chairs were worth about five dollars a pair, and every FNS facility had plenty of them.

Handmaking cane-bottom chairs – *FNS photo, courtesy of Univ. of Kentucky archives.*

Cash was so scarce and it was so difficult to get to Hyden Citizens Bank during business hours, that when FNS payroll checks went out, they'd get passed from one person to another, each endorsing it and paying their debts. "They were business-size checks – the longest checks I'd ever seen," recalled Mrs. Breckinridge. "When the bank sent the paid checks back to us, signatures covered the entire backside. It read like a telephone directory of the county."

In the fall, when the weather cooled off so meats wouldn't spoil, it was butchering time. If the family could afford it, they finished their animals on corn to take away their gaminess from the wild beechnuts, acorns and whatever else they'd foraged in the woods. The best time to butcher was traditionally during the "old moon in November." Men would "gang up" and help each other. One man would kill a half a dozen animals, and the others would cut up and hang the meat for smoking. The lard was rendered and kept for making soap.

Ginseng and mayapple grow in the Kentucky climate, but slowly. The roots, dug up and dried, were a profitable export but could only be harvested in small quantities. Ginseng was used for many ailments, especially lung complaints. Mayapple root was used as a cathartic. People were secretive about plantings of both medicinal herbs, because they needed to sell what they could in town to buy shoes, coffee or flour.

Donna was on district out of Flat Creek, checking up on a postpartum. Mother and week-old baby were doing well. The cabin was neat, smelled of fried pork, and there were pans of cornbread cooling on the table. A lard can of milk was hanging above the stove, clabbering for buttermilk. All seemed to be well with the family.

"Miss Donna, we aim to settle our account fer you helpin' the least 'un bein' borned," the husband said. "I'll have something fer you directly." He left the house.

Donna finished bathing and dressing the baby, and went out. As she threw her saddlebags over Jefferson, she spotted the man preparing to chop the head off a turkey.

"Oh! Please don't kill him!" shouted Donna.

The man stopped and looked at her, puzzled.

"Put him in this feed sack and I'll take him alive!"

She pulled a feed sack from where she'd rolled and tucked it behind her saddle. With some difficulty, they put the huge bird in the sack and tied it shut it with a short piece of rawhide.

"My horse doesn't tolerate blood of any kind," Donna explained. "I'll take my chances hauling the bird home alive." She mounted. With a wary eye on the sack, Jefferson took a few side steps before letting the man hand it up to her. It was thrashing and squawking something awful. Jefferson's ears went back and he swished his tail up and down while Bucky barked excitedly.

"Would you rather I should fetch you a possum? Hit'd just play dead."

"No, thank you. I'll take my chances with the turkey," Donna repeated.

"It was the longest seven miles I've ever ridden," Donna told the nurses one evening at Hyden after dinner. Everyone laughed, but they agreed the turkey made for much better eating than a rank possum. Sure enough, like Mrs. Breckinridge had said, sometimes you'd need a feed sack to bring home payment. "It's the only time Jefferson broke his gait. Even the snake falling on us from out of the tree didn't put him off his pace like that angry sack of feathers!"

The system of a grain cooperative worked well in Appalachia. Usually there was one family within a day's mule ride who owned a corn mill. It would be situated on a creek where a head of water could be controlled to power the mill. After harvest, and after the ears had dried enough to shell, people brought their corn for grinding into meal. The mill owner kept part of the ground meal for payment.

Mountain people made their own sorghum molasses for sweetener. They planted sugar cane in rows like corn. When the cane tops ripened and turned brown, it was ready for harvest. The whole family would work the harvest and the crush. The tops were cut off the stalks and the tough fibers were stripped from the cane. Then it was thrown into a round bin-type mill. A crushing wheel was driven by a horse or mule walking circles around the bin. The juice was collected in wash tubs, which were then placed over an open fire to boil out the water. The froth was stirred off while the syrup thickened into clear, rich brown molasses.

A stir-off — *FNS photo, courtesy of Univ. of Kentucky archives.*

Some miles from the Flat Creek Clinic, a stir-off was taking place. Abigail and the other children had peeled off their coats in the warm autumn afternoon. She stood near the tub of boiling molasses and peered at it through the steam.

"Not too thick, and not too thin now," their father said to the little girl. "When it blubbers up sheep's eye-lookin' bubbles, you let me know." He unhitched the mule and led it off toward the barn. "If'n yer good, Mommy will bake you some tough jack candy!" This delighted the children. Molasses could be pulled like taffy or baked to a glistening texture like hard candy.

"Hit's ready!" little Abigail shouted. The other children were raking up the cane fiber and tops to feed the hogs. Their mother was inside with the baby, and their father wasn't finished with the mule yet. Abigail, teetering on tiptoes, reached up with the wooden paddle to stir off the last of the steaming froth.

The nurses at Flat Creek were taking care of the last few people when they heard shouting from outside. They opened the door and a foursome of people approached, carrying a home-made pole stretcher. On it was a little girl who'd just been burned at their stir-off. The tub had tipped on its pinnings and boiling syrup scalded her. By the time they got her to the creek, she was already burned, they explained to the nurses.

"It's Abigail," Donna said as they brought her to the cot in the clinic. The child lay on her back, her eyes glassy and expressionless. The nurses examined peeling, angry second-and third-degree burns on the front of her legs from her thighs to her ankles. Syrup is so cloying, once it contacts the skin, it continues to burn. The nurses sent the father on a horse to the nearest telephone to notify Hyden to have someone meet them at the road in the FNS Jeep. As they delicately put salve and gauze over her burns, the nurses feared the little girl may go into shock. They kept her warm and gave her a stimulant and prepared her for transportation to the hospital. The housekeeper served bean soup and biscuits to everyone as they sat quietly in the clinic waiting for the arrival of the vehicle. It was dark when they heard it honk at the road below the center, and with the nurses walking alongside, the four carried the girl to the road and loaded her in the Jeep. A nurse from Hyden rode along and sat beside Abigail for the trip to the hospital.

The nurses were terribly upset. Burns! They were a too-frequent affair. Children were expected to be as capable as adults. But little girls' cotton dresses caught fire over wood-burning stoves. Their little arms got seared by frying grease. They tipped tubs of boiling syrup as they teetered trying to make themselves tall enough to help.

They don't spend many years just being children, Donna thought.

We Can't Run a Hospital
Without Horseshoes

"It was hard to convince those in the highest levels in Washington, D.C. that horseshoes are essential to childbirth."

— Mary Breckinridge

"Miz Breckinridge, I jus' checked our supply o' horseshoes like you axed, and after I redd up all the barns and sheds, I only come up with one keg o' shoes."

"What does that mean, Ellery? How long before we will need more?"

"I s'pect iron's gonna be harder to come by . . ." he trailed off, rubbing his broad chin. "We have a bad chance o' changin' that . . ."

"Don't give me theories, give me facts, please, Ellery. I need to know what our needs are so I can work on the most critical. Last week it was diapers. If it's horseshoes this week, I need to know."

The Frontier Nursing Service was probably the only health care service in the nation with a forge shed and on-staff blacksmith. You'd have looked far and wide to find another nursing headquarters that had to deal with the disposal of manure and the breeding rhythms of cows, or routinely listed horseshoes and replacement riding tack and harness on its supplies list.

Ellery and his forge were essential for all kinds of repairs anywhere they were needed. Ellery's most important job was keeping their three dozen horses fit for duty. It only took a month or so to use up a gross of horseshoes. "Well, Miz Breckinridge, I stopped shoein' the mules a long time ago. They c'n get along without. Fer the horses, we have only about a month and a half's worth. Unless you want I should go more than four weeks between shoein'. But I think we ortent not do that."

"No, Ellery, I do not advise that. We cannot jeopardize our horses' feet."

Horseback was the only way the nurses could serve many of the families. Horses were still used on more than eighty per cent of their travel out of necessity. Mrs. Breckinridge had seen more than once in the current week's reports that a nurse had brought someone to the Hyden hospital on her horse. In one urgent case it was a twelve-year old boy with double pneumonia.

"And with the rationing of gasoline and rubber for tires, the horses are ever more important to our work," she concluded.

The FNS was rated high priority for getting most supplies, but shortages nagged the staff and nearly throttled much of its function. Iron for horseshoes went instead into war materiel. Before they ran out of horseshoes, Mrs. Breckinridge urgently planned a different kind of outreach journey. This time, she intended to convince the United States Congress to direct some iron away from the battleship and tank factories and in her direction instead.

Mrs. Breckinridge was a personal friend of Eleanor Roosevelt. Over tea at the White House, she held the First Lady's attention with stories of her FNS nurses riding horseback up and down the hollows delivering babies in cabins wallpapered with old newspaper, while hot lard crackled in a skillet, and chickens on the porch pecked bugs from beneath handmade rocking chairs. She left nothing out. She talked about her nurses saving the lives of mothers and babies by the light of kerosene lamps, while the rivers rose in tides that cut them off from any other medical help. "Without horseshoes, we can't deliver babies; without diapers we can't properly care for them either!"

Nurse rides through the Middle Fork
because there are few roads — *courtesy of FNS.*

Nurses dismount and cross swinging bridge on foot to make a home visit — *courtesy of FNS.*

Typical home visit — *FNS photo, courtesy of Univ. of Kentucky archives.*

Mrs. Roosevelt was a leader among the Frontier Nursing Service's Washington sponsors, but her personal interest in this wartime supply struggle was even more valuable right then. Perhaps Mrs. Breckinridge's approach was a little out of the ordinary for government business, but it worked, and Congress came through in 1943 with the notification that iron would be made available for horseshoe production. "I used every tactic I could think of," she said, recalling the mission.

High priority status didn't solve the diaper shortage either. Looms that had been turning out soft white cotton birds-eye for diapers were refitted to turn out military burlap. Diaper fabric was rationed out at five yards per customer. The nurses had to resort to diapering the hospital babies in used linens. But the worn fabric was not suitable for use out in the districts because it didn't hold up to folks' crude washing methods. A plea went out to all FNS donors, and earnest patrons bought up every diaper or birds-eye yardage they could to send to Wendover. The *Detroit Free Press* reported a "burgeoning black market in diapers." Mrs. Breckinridge never knew how much her generous patrons paid when they managed to find some. She was just relieved when boxes arrived full of diapers, and new white material that could be sewn into diapers.

Mrs. Breckinridge was also on an ardent search of a different kind. Another war-related shortage nabbed Dr. Kooser who had served as FNS Medical Director for twelve years. The Navy needed him, and his departure affected the FNS deeply. "We sent him off to the Navy's Medical Reserve Corps with a smile, when our hearts were heavy," Mrs. Breckinridge said. Her search for a replacement "involved correspondence a foot high," because trained medical professionals were in demand for the war around the globe. A small hospital and clinic network in rural Kentucky was of no concern to a war machine stretched thin.

It wasn't only doctors who were plucked from civilian service. An October 1942 government bulletin stated, "It is now generally recognized that nursing presents one of the critical shortages of woman-power in the war effort." The military wanted a large roster of nurses to draw upon if the need arose. All nurses under forty-five years of age, with no children under fourteen years old, were required to register for classification with the War Manpower

Commission, which was similar to the draft board. The objective of the Procurement and Assignment Center was "to procure nurses to meet the needs of the Armed Forces, having due consideration of civilian nursing needs."

There were three basic classifications: Class One, Available; Class Four, Essential; and Class Five, Not Available Because of Physical Disability or Age. An "Available" 1-A classification obligated nurses to contact the Red Cross Nurse Recruitment Center immediately and apply to the Army or Navy Nurse Corps.

"You and I haven't a chance for Class Five, so it's important that we convince the Commission that we're '*Class Four essential*' to the health of our Kentucky civilians," Evelyn said to Donna. "If they could only see us working on any day or night, they'd see how *essential* we are to our communities. They'd send each of us a dozen roses and *run* back to Washington!"

The two women asked Ardice to help them complete their registration forms. Two weeks later, official letters from the War Manpower Commission arrived for them, and with much anxiety they opened their envelopes. Scanning the letters quickly for the critical classification that could thrust them into Red Cross military service, they saw the 4-A, "Essential" status in the second paragraph. They were at present filling an "essential civilian need." They could remain "unless the supply of 1-A nurses became exhausted," the letter stated.

"I don't think we have to worry about leaving FNS for now," Evelyn said, with relief in her voice. "I'm praying the war is over before we are needed. What good is sending nurses who are already exhausted to help the ones who are becoming exhausted already?"

The war affected people of all ages. Military-age Kentuckians were enlisting in the armed forces, as well as migrating beyond the mountains to fill good-paying jobs. Defense contractors were straining to produce equipment and supplies for the military and wanted mountain men with their strong work ethic. The radio and newspapers announced a national scrap metal drive, and American children were challenged to do their part to help the Allies by collecting scrap so it could be hauled to foundries and made into bombs. Hyden seventh graders scoured yards, creek beds and fields and came up with *four tons* of it. The newspaper reported that "as a result of their victory in the scrap metal contest, they were awarded Defense Stamps" which could be collected and turned in for U. S. savings bonds.

The local newspapers ran government public service announcements with the attention-getting headline, "Discarded Silk Stockings Keep U. S. Guns Booming." Women were asked to send in their used silk stockings as part of the "Victory Parade." Stockings could be remade into gunpowder bags for the primer charge on large caliber guns. Silk burns completely, leaving no residue. That meant that gun barrels did not require frequent cleaning between discharges, and "guns can be re-charged without loss of valuable time."

The nurses saw the irony in that appeal showing up in local papers.

"What Leslie County woman even *owns* a single pair of silk stockings?" Evelyn asked.

"Besides, we never discard *anything* around here!" Donna added.

"We're sorry, Uncle Sam . . . now, if you were asking for *cow manure*. . ." The women all laughed.

While the rest of the nation sent in their surplus silk stockings and learned to live without a selection of red meats in their grocery stores, Kentucky mountain families were hardly affected. From generations of living off their land they'd perfected ways to sustain themselves. If they could grow it, they could preserve it. There were no freezers. They sulphured apples. Sliced apples were layered in a barrel. A dish of hot coals was placed in the barrel with a sprinkle of sulphur on it and the barrel was covered with a blanket and left for a few days. This preserved the apples' color and flavor. After a little soaking, the apples plumped back and made tasty pies, cobblers or applesauce. Women canned berries, pears and plums; they dried shucky beans and soaked corn kernels for a few days in lye water until the husks and germ came off, then swelled into filling hominy. The men preserved butchered hogs over smoldering hickory bark; hens supplied fresh eggs much of the year, and when the old hens stopped laying, their tough meat was simmered into stew. Whether there was a war on or not, cows gave milk, squash and potatoes grew, and hogs fattened up.

Kentucky sent an out-of-proportion number of soldiers to fight. Ironically, for some at home, life improved because men from the Kentucky mountains who received battle pay could send allotments home. The modest checks helped wives, mothers, sisters and brothers endure while their men fought on a hostile continent or South Pacific island half a world away.

Kentucky mountaineers had always bartered skills like woodworking, whitewashing and post-hole digging for essentials other families had in surplus. That mode of commerce continued as always. Floods and droughts mattered more to these people, and could create food shortages more severe than running out of war ration stamps. The rationing of store-bought supplies meant they just stretched the flour, sugar, coffee and leather goods a little thinner to make it to next month's distribution of rationing coupons. The coupons themselves became trading stock.

Shoes were scarce, and a family might have just one pair to pass around to their children. They alternated "shoe days" and would go barefoot on their off-days.

Regardless of the scarcity of food in their pantries, the people graciously offered the nurses nourishment if they stayed through a mealtime.

"I've never met any people who can kill, dress out and fry a chicken any faster," Donna told Evelyn one day. "And nothing goes to waste. Have you been offered a chicken gizzard sandwich yet? Like possum pie, it's tolerable if you're hungry enough!"

Three Dollar-a-Day Career

"Another Angel in Heaven — Sept. 8, 1911 to April 14, 1912 "

— inscription on gravestone, Leslie County, Kentucky

*B*efore the highlanders began to accept the modern notion of hygiene, vaccines, and other ways to prevent disease, their most common home approach to wellness was frequent "purgings." Drug stores sold a lot of Black Draught laxative, a mixture of mostly epsom salts and magnesium. Castor oil was another standby remedy. For anyone suffering any sort of malaise, swallowing a tablespoonful would release from the bowels what was thought to be the trouble. Their homes were never without mixtures to clear the digestive tract, and remedies to "stop the runnin' off."

Black Draught was doubly handy to have around, because it was pretty effective when the cow or mule got colic, which could be deadly. Losing the milk cow or plow mule was a serious financial setback.

Typhoid was a common killer. The disease was spread through contact with contaminated feces, usually traceable to privies or animal pens too close to the water supply, or careless attention to hygiene around dirty diapers. An infected person could be a carrier without showing symptoms, and could contaminate food, infecting their whole family. In a campaign to reduce typhoid, the Works Progress Administration launched a program in the 1930s to upgrade sanitation facilities for the mountain dwellings. If the homeowner provided the lumber and nails, the government work party would construct a latrine on the property. New little outhouses popped up in the clearings. Some families preferred to put the handy little buildings to use storing their coal or animal feed, sometimes even animals, and continued using their old outhouses.

Mrs. Breckinridge was passionate about pure water and keeping it separate from animal and human waste. She revered

Florence Nightingale and studied her success cleaning up hospitals in Europe during the 1800s. Nightingale exposed dreadfully unsanitary conditions in hospitals. Injured soldiers were dying of diseases they were exposed to *in* the hospital. Nightingale motivated authorities to bury dead animals that were contaminating the water supply, and improve hygiene and sewage treatment. She was successful fighting dysentery, typhoid and cholera. Her modest publications left an indelible mark on Mrs. Breckinridge, and became a cornerstone of the FNS public health agenda.

Trachoma was rampant in the area. It's a persistent and contagious eye infection that's spread with dirty linens and handkerchiefs. If not cured, it causes cornea damage and impaired vision[2].

When Donna visited her families out on district, over a cup of tea the woman might share her knowledge of family remedies and superstitions. Donna was always respectful, knowing that for generations, that was all these people had.

One woman told her that there had been a shooting death years ago in her hollow, and "Fer years, people was skeert to come up here alone. They swore that ever' time they passed through, they heer'd voices and a 'hant' jumped on the back o' their mule!"

One afternoon at the Hyden dorm, Donna shared some stories she'd heard, and the nurses became animated, adding their own anecdotes.

"I can understand the teas made of bark, roots and herbs. But for measles when they made pills of sheep dung . . . " One nurse shuddered.

"They made poultices of eye-stinging tinctures to treat breathing problems . . ." another chimed in. "How about home-made turpentine? Seems a shock like that would take your breath away!"

Folk remedies usually came from the woods; some even came from woods creatures.

"Did you know that for colds they'd make salve of polecat grease? How would you like to be the unlucky one who had to gather it from the skunk's backside?!"

"Don't be silly! I understand that first they would drown the poor animal!"

[2] The U. S. Public Health Department set up a trachoma clinic in Richmond, Kentucky, to serve the region. The FNS had become so effective at preventing the eye disease, that the treatment center closed in 1950.

"I heard that for croup, they'd cut the core out of an onion, fill it with sulphur, and roast the onion for awhile. The patient would drink the squeezings from it."

"The treatments didn't *cure* anything. Once you began to recover naturally, stopping those awful treatments made you feel like you were better!"

"Just the dread of the cure was powerful medicine!"

Some laughed.

But it was no laughing matter to answer a call to a home where the children were suffering from diphtheria. It was the disease Mrs. Breckinridge and the nurses dreaded most. It is highly contagious and can spread quickly with a cough or sneeze, or handling contaminated toys and clothing. A person can carry the disease without showing symptoms. A child could become infected at school, return to his own home crowded with several small children, and infect them all. A horse-serum vaccine wasn't available until the 1940s, and the FNS nurses did their best to treat the children without antibiotics. The tiny children could not express they were not feeling well. By the time symptoms showed, and the nurse was called, it was often too late. The bacteria develop a membrane that restricts breathing – "a risin' in the throat" it was called with great dread. A lot of prayers went unanswered as its dreadful symptoms strangled children to death. Babies died before they left their first footprint on the earth, leaving nothing more than little granite markers in the family cemeteries.

The nurses saw disease caused by malnutrition. It's a long stretch between fall harvest and when the tender spring greens shoot up from the waking earth. Winter diets were deficient in many nutrients. Pellagra and toxemia were pernicious maladies. Both diseases are especially risky for pregnant women whose bodies are sacificing vital nutrients to the gestating baby. A diet heavy in corn gives the feeling of fullness, yet does not provide an essential level of niacin. Pellagra starts as a soreness in the mouth and red patches on the skin, and can eventually affect the nerves and brain. Toxemia occurs in the absence of fresh foods, which causes mineral deficiency. Now termed "Pre-eclampsia," it comes on as high blood pressure, swelling, and high levels of protein in the urine. That's the indication that the kidneys are leaking valuable proteins that should be nourishing the placenta. It no longer nourishes the baby, who is then at risk for serious problems. If the condition worsens into "eclampsia," the woman can suffer seizures and a safe delivery for both baby and mother is truly in jeopardy.

"We must continue to educate the families on the importance of good pre-natal care," Mrs. Breckinridge always said. "If we can monitor the pregnancies, we can avoid the risks." By the time Donna was delivering babies on her own, Mrs. Breckinridge's theory had been solidly proven. Her colleagues were making a difference. The maternal death rate had dropped to about one third of that throughout the United States.[3]

FNS nurses didn't dwell on the fact that they were saving mothers' lives and keeping people alive who'd suffered illness and accidents. They just daily carried out their duties, enjoying an occasional dinner together at the Hyden dorm between weeks serving at their outposts or the hospital.

A nurse's sense of fulfillment came from the bedside, with the strong squeeze of a patient's hand, or from the eyes of a recovering child after their fever had broken – a fever that may have sucked the life from them, had the nurse not brought her modern cures in her saddlebags. The statistics were proof of success, but to the nurses, those numbers were abstract – just figures on paper. The real reward was the new mother and pink nursing baby lying on a corn husk pallet beneath a clean coverlid. Leaving the peaceful home knowing the baby and mother were on their way to health and wellness was a payoff beyond anything you could measure.

No one in the Frontier Nursing Service – including founder Mary Breckinridge – was paid over one hundred and fifty dollars per month, the bottom income bracket according to the Bureau of Internal Revenue. Meal and laundry deductions amounted to one-fourth of their gross pay. If they ever really figured it out, the nurses earned about three dollars a day, based on a seven-day week. What sustained them was knowing that their small cadre of trained nurse-midwives was dramatically improving local health standards and saving the lives of mothers and babies.

[3] At the end their first 10,000 live births (1925-1955) the FNS lost 9.1 mothers due to delivery causes; among white women in the U. S. during the same period, the average rate was 34 per 10,000. (Statistics published in 1968-1969 FNS *Quarterly Bulletin.*)

The nurses could take every other weekend off and would alternate on-call responsibilities. On their weekends off they sometimes rode the bus to London or Manchester, or just rode their horses to the dorm at Hyden to catch up on reading and socializing. After a spring rain, it was fun to hunt through the damp woods for "land fish" or morel mushrooms. The little elfin treasures added a wonderful flavor to scrambled eggs. When dry, hot weather finally came, they often packed a picnic and rode to a new place.

On a sunny April day Donna and some of the nurses prepared a picnic. It was such a pleasure to enjoy the fresh spring mountain air with no chance for an emergency call. They rode past a well-known family's cemetery, stopping for a moment to look over the weathered gravestones in the shadows of a few blossoming plum trees. One marker caught their attention, with dates that were much too close together. The math was easy. This child did not live a full year.

"Another angel in heaven," one of them read from the inscription on the gravestone.

They spotted other markers with similar dates. They stood in silence for a few moments, sharing a wave of sympathy. Breaking the silence, one of them said, "Probably diphtheria, wouldn't you guess?"

They were working to prevent diseases like diphtheria from choking the life from so many. Donna felt a soft sense of pride, knowing that she was part of a gentle power bringing wellness to these people she had become so fond of.

She walked back to her horse with the other women. "We all want the angels here on earth," she thought. "I think we are doing something to make sure their time in Heaven is a long way off."

Coffins Already Built

D aniel was unknown to the nurses at the Brutus Clinic. He had never registered himself or his family with the Frontier Nursing Service. Donna had learned of him only when his wife Willa appeared at the clinic to request help. She approached the building in a bent-forward way, and the creases between her eyebrows told of her exhaustion.

"He's very poorly, but his mind is turned away from you'uns," said Willa. "When he couldn't get shed of his cough, I wanted to call by to tell you, but he was ag'in' it."

"Let's get your information added to our records, so we can begin helping you," Donna said, gently putting her hand on the woman's sinewy arm, to guide her to a chair. The woman had walked several miles to reach the clinic, wearing worn men's oxford shoes and no stockings. A hickory cloth jacket smelling of coal oil smoke hung over her faded cotton dress.

Donna started to understand more about Daniel as Willa answered some basic questions. Her husband "didn't want no medical attention from the fotched-on women" of the Frontier Nursing Service. Instead, he chose to doctor himself with drugstore cures and what medicinals the woods around his home had to offer. Willa was caring for him with white oak bark tea and a hot poultice she made by soaking a square of yarn cloth in turpentine. If there was no turpentine, she used lard and coal oil instead. She heated it on the wood stove and laid it on his chest. Either pungent concoction held the heat and relieved his feeling of congestion for awhile. Donna suspected he was using another common remedy – whiskey. When mixed with a bit of honey or molasses, it made a tempting cough syrup. Predictably, Daniel's breathing and weakness had only worsened.

"He ain't been able to work cuttin' posts since May." Willa added that she and the children had taken on his chores around the place.

Before she left the clinic, Willa drew Donna away from the others waiting in the clinic and said to her, "you belong to know that I see'd that he was coughin' blood."

"How I wish these people would let us help them sooner," Donna thought as she marked his name in her book, followed by "*Pulmonary tuberculosis suspected.*"

"These folks are strong and able, but not unconquerable by disease with their poor diet and work-worn bodies," she said to Nora, the other Brutus nurse, "and it's hard to overcome habits that are so dug in." Generations of pioneers swore by the claimed healing powers of smoking dried life-everlasting leaves to ease a cough. But this bygone remedy had no real benefit for Daniel. Instead, his reliance on dubious cures just delayed proper medical care. This disease was called "consumption" for a terrible and proved-out reason. Once a person showed real symptoms, their body was being consumed from the inside.

Tuberculosis was also called the "white plague" as epidemics made murderous sweeps through Europe and England during the Industrial Age. Living and working long hours in close quarters without fresh air or hot wash water created conditions in which bacteria thrived. In 1815, while they were mechanizing their world, one in four Europeans was infected with some form of this primitive illness. The tiniest speck of sputum from the touch of someone's hand or being in a room where someone sneezed could become a death sentence. And there was no defense against it.

Survivors of the disease naturally produced offspring with some immunity, and immigrants to this country brought inside them a natural resistance. But mountain homes in the hollows of southeast Kentucky were not wholesome, sunlit places where fresh breezes fluffed the air. In dark, close cabin interiors, large families shared fusty air that harbored tuberculosis bacteria. Even raw milk, thought to be wholesome, was a haven for the bacteria. Lodging in a host with an immune system weakened by the fatigue of a hard life, the bacteria could hopelessly damage lungs or other organs.

In pulmonary cases, the disease began with a nagging cough. The common defense tactic was patent medicine advertised in the local papers. Bold type shouted at readers to "Beware Coughs That Hang On." Creomulsion, one ad promised, "relieves promptly because it goes to the seat of the trouble to help loosen and expel germ-laden phlegm and aid nature to soothe and heal raw, tender inflamed bronchial mucous membranes!" This sure-fire cure was a lot more desirable than medical attention, especially when the closest hospital might be seventeen miles away and accessible only by foot or mule, through creek beds and over steep ridges.

Because there were no antibiotics, the best strategy was avoidance of the illness. Frontier nurses tried to educate families about its very contagious nature. Even though it added chores to their daily work, heating raw milk and having plenty of hot water around for washing would keep them healthy. If a person showed symptoms, attempts at a quarantine would be made to isolate the sick from the healthy. This arrangement was not easy in homes known crudely as "three rooms and a path."

News spread that a miracle cure was saving lives by overpowering bacterial disease. But production of the new drug, Penicillin, was strained by the demands of the war. Troops were given supply priority. After what seemed to the Frontier Nursing staff like an eternal wait for the medicine, the War Supply Board finally authorized a certain number of Penicillin doses to be available for American civilian use. The FNS cached the medicine as if it were more valuable than gold.

Donna prepared for Daniel's home visit. She carefully measured out one precious dose of the new antibiotic and tucked the vial between some linens in her saddlebag to protect it during the long ride. Its effects on tuberculosis were unknown, but Donna was willing to try it. Daniel needed nothing short of a miracle.

Donna found the home and approached it in her usual manner, hollering out a clear "hello-o-o" from the border fence. Willa appeared, pausing a long moment for her eyes to adjust to the outside summer daylight. Donna saw fear in her drawn face and deep-set eyes. Maybe even a little shame.

The woman motioned her in, and Donna set her bags on the crude floor. A child brought in a large bundle of rhubarb stalks, and seeing the nurse, silently set it down and slipped back outdoors.

Donna saw a kettle half-full of neatly-diced rhubarb. The woman set a tea kettle on the wood stove and placed two cups on the table. Donna was encouraged by the gesture of welcome and acceptance. Willa fidgeted with the spoons and rolled the ends of her apron sash around her red-stained fingers while the water came to a boil. Donna made friendly small talk, sensing that the woman needed to build up her confidence. She would allow as much time as Willa needed to take the lead on any conversation that was to occur.

As they sipped tea, Donna heard sounds from outside like someone building something out of wood. There were no voices. She heard sawing, a pause, then a moment of riving, then hammering.

Willa finally spoke up. "Miss Donna, I know you are here to check on Dan'l, but we all come to a hard choice and he ain't 'zactly here right now."

"Willa, I need to begin his treatment if we want him to have a better chance of overcoming his sickness. I'll take care of him whenever he is ready."

"Well . . . Miss Donna, hit's hard to say it, but we come to a choice and set him up outside fer the sake o' the young'uns."

Donna searched Willa's eyes for more clues. "That's fine, I'll take my bag to him and it won't take long."

They stepped out onto the porch, and Donna's gaze followed the woman's outstretched hand, pointing at a tree near the edge of the clearing. There was a crude board structure leaning out from the crotch in an old tree, eight or so feet above the ground. "I heer'd of others getting the TB, but I think now we're experiencing it out," Willa said simply.

They had made a quarantine shelter for Daniel to live in. A bucket tied to a rope was strung over a branch to elevate his food and other needs to him. A slop bucket was also attached to a rope and looped over a different branch.

As Donna absorbed the situation, she realized that the construction she'd heard was probably the building of Daniel's coffin.

She approached the tree and called to him. Daniel's face eventually appeared, pale, unshaven, his listless eyes sunken in their sockets. He looked sixty years old. It was hard to believe this woodsman's hale torso had filled a size-fifteen flannel shirt not very long ago.

"I've come to help you, Daniel. I have a new treatment here that has helped many others."

"No need to waste that on me, miss," the weak voice said. He lay back where Donna could not see him. "Nate is taking care of the only thing I need . . . but thank you, miss."

Donna made a mental note of everything, so she could record it in the clinic's records. It was plain to see that the right thing to do was to honor his wish and save the antibiotic for someone else. One dose at this advanced stage of the illness would have no healing effect.

"Don't think ill of us, Miss Donna," Willa softy appealed as the nurse prepared to leave. "I know hit's a bad way to treat a man below forty years of age. But when an un-chosen thing like this happens, all that c'n be done is fer kin to build a proper coffin."

The family's response was to wall off the threat like they would sandbag the rising waters of a flood. They had accepted that there would be unstoppable suffering, then death. Donna knew that Daniel's illness would soon cause his infected and hemorrhaging lungs to fail; he would suffocate from lack of oxygen. He would leave a weary widow and four fatherless children. The family would face it stoically, the same way they would face a crop-flattening hailstorm or a lightning fire.

For the last one hundred and thirty years, the rest of the western world had been making headway in the battle against TB. Vaccines arrived in Leslie County bringing hope of stamping out the disease. But it was too late to help Daniel. "Would he have been willing to accept our help?" Donna wondered. "All up and down these hollows they fight TB in silence, risking the health of their families, then go untreated until they're beyond any miracle," she agonized.

Struggling for some kind of reconciliation, Donna decided the tree was probably better than treatment in some "civilized" place where the poor and sick were isolated in sanatoriums where living conditions were as shoddy as prisons. A tree house in the backyard had its advantages. Donna had to let go of her frustration at not being able to help. She gave Willa a bit of hygiene advice to keep the disease from infecting anyone else in the household. She left antiseptic soap and some strong pain medication for Daniel, if he wanted to use it.

As she secured her saddlebags and untied her horse, Donna thought about Nate, whose way of helping his dying brother was to build him a sturdy yellow poplar coffin in the sunshine right there in plain sight. She mounted Jefferson and as she turned slowly away from the cabin, she spotted the family cemetery up the hill. Stone markers pointed feebly to the sky from their skewed settings in the tall grass at the upper edge of the clearing.

Practical folks buried their dead well above any place the floods could reach.

Cold Creeks and Thump Kegs

"In your country, like the land of promise, flowing with milk and honey, a land of brooks of water, of fountains and depths, that spring out of valleys and hills, a land of wheat and barley, and all kinds of fruits, you shall eat bread without scarceness, and not lack any thing in it; where you are neither chilled with the cold of Capricorn nor scorched with the burning of Cancer . . . thus your country [is] favored with the smiles of heaven . . . "

— John Filson, *The Discovery, Settlement and Present State of Kentucke,*
published in 1784. (A popular guidebook of the day)

The highlands of Leslie, Perry and Clay counties never fulfilled the promise Mr. Filson so poetically described in his archaic guidebook. In 1930, Mary B. Willeford of Texas[4] conducted a detailed survey of the economic condition of the area, for her doctoral thesis. Her findings were bleak. Family tracts were typically about ten acres, but only a few were suitable for planting. If they could patch together four acres' worth to harvest, they were doing better than most. Steep hills sprinkled with hardwoods yielded some timber and forage for their hogs. Half of the families in the area earned less than one thousand dollars a year. Their subsistence farming was buffeted by flood and drought. In drought years, they reaped more nourishment by shooting and making stew out of the squirrels that pestered their corn. Although the country was not "favored with the smiles of Heaven," Heaven did seem to smile on fertile women, because mothers averaged nine births. As soon as the children's fingers were big enough to plant seeds, pull weeds, or snap the tips off bushels of beans, they worked alongside their parents. But providing the things they could not produce themselves required some kind of income.

---

[4] Willeford served as an FNS nurse in 1926, eventually becoming assistant director.

To be truthful in reporting her findings, Ms. Willeford had to mention an enterprise very important to some familes' incomes: "There is another source of revenue not considered herein. The making and selling of 'moonshine whiskey' is a more or less common practice in this area."

Not wishing to risk her life in further examination of this backwoods industry, she prudently left the topic alone. "It is impossible, however, to obtain any reliable figures on the amount of such business conducted or the profit derived in this way," she discreetly concluded.

What the area lacked in opportunity, it made up for with an abundance of fast-running, cold creek water, firewood, corn and seclusion. Add to the mix a nation willing to pay cash for a product that multiplied the value of a bushel of corn, and it was no wonder a lot of "white mule" traveled out of the mountains not on hooves but in jugs.

Liquor production has always been a large part of Kentucky's culture and economy. In 1792, a Lexington tavern was the meeting place where the commonwealth's government was organized. By then, there were already distilleries in production. Over libations and debate, Kentucky became our fifteenth state. Today, Kentucky produces more than ninety-five per cent of the world's bourbon, caramel-colored corn whiskey that starts out the same way moonshine does, then is aged a couple of years in charred oak barrels. This tames its kick. The longer it ages, the smoother it gets. The brand name "Old Grand-Dad" suggests that distilling is a respected part of family culture.

The Prohibition was long gone, but Leslie County citizens voted repeatedly to keep the little county dry. The most recent vote had occurred in February, 1943. The results were two-to-one to keep liquor out. But in the hollows along a few creeks, thump kegs kept busy distilling liquor, usually under the cover of dark. Neighbors didn't see moonshiners as morally wrong, since they laid low and bothered no one. Villainy was squarely placed on bootleggers and government revenue agents.

When Mrs. Breckinridge discussed it, she began by posing this question: "What would you do if your corn only fetched a dollar a bushel for human or livestock food, but at thirty or forty dollars for the same amount of corn you could support your family by running it through your still?" She let her nurses ponder that rhetorical question. "You are to hear nothing, see nothing and say nothing," she reminded them. They were to remain neutral. Mrs. Breckinridge understood early on that in order to gain safe access and confidence of the locals, this was essential.

Mrs. Breckinridge was sometimes asked about Kentucky's reputation for moonshining in her fundraising meetings beyond the mountains. "During the prohibition we dreaded the federal agents, and we feared the bootleggers, but not one of us has ever been afraid of a moonshiner, then or now," she explained. "Only one problem concerned us: The unknown potency of liquor coming out of the unregulated producers and the safety of those consuming it."

Corn mash was soaked in a barrel with yeast, and sometimes sugar was added. As it "worked," or fermented, it pushed vapor into a cap, then into a tube that ran into the "thump keg" – named for the thumping noise as the first distilling impurities passed into it. The hot vapor siphoned itself through the "worm," the copper tube that spiraled through another container of cold creek water, to create condensation. The condensation was caught in a keg. It was clear as water and potent, and earned nicknames like "pop-skull," "bust-head," "rot gut," "white mule" or "white lightning."

Why were the feds or "revenuers" so despised?

That sentiment had its genesis after the Civil War. Post-war Reconstruction encouraged new enterprise, so moonshine operations sprouted up in what a Charleston, North Carolina reporter called the nation's "dark corners." The FNS service area had plenty of those. U. S. Revenue agents were delegates of the victorious Union and were expected to collect taxes from whiskey manufacturers, large and small.

But the moonshiners, having sympathized with the Confederates, had other ideas. After the war, taxes to pay for Reconstruction were slapped on distillers in the South. Most of the tax collectors, disparagingly called "revenoors," were local Unionists. Folks who had remained loyal to the Confederacy had enough trouble feeding their families with the little bit of income they could brew out of their corn and grain. They resented their neighbors and former friends collecting taxes for a cause they still hadn't reconciled with. It was a bitter pill. Paradoxically, during Prohibition, Kentuckians were prosecuted for producing something that much of the nation prized. Notorious moonshiner Lewis R. Redmond shot and killed a revenue agent, and staged a well-publicized rescue of his gang members from jails in the Blue Ridge Mountains. A pulp novel romanticized the golden-haired, handsome desperado, reinforcing the Appalachian aversion to federal authority.

"Isn't it exciting!" Evelyn exclaimed at dinner. She and Ginger had just returned to the nurses' headquarters from the Brutus outpost on Bullskin Creek. "Ginger and I were out on district and we heard strange noises coming from the brush, like blowing across a Coca-Cola bottle. Ginger said to just keep riding, and act like I didn't hear anything. It was then I saw the still. A few men stood around, watching us pass. If they hadn't been there, I would never have noticed it. Ginger said to look straight ahead, and just keep talking. When we got back to the clinic, Ginger explained that the sound we heard was a 'gun telephone.' The men were signaling along the trail so we could pass by safely."

Ginger interrupted her. "Evelyn, you think you saw a still, but you didn't," she insisted with a furtive look. "You did *not* see a still!"

The gun telephone was an improvised way to communicate that a friendly person was riding through, and to let them pass. When a man recognized two women on horseback as FNS nurses, he blew across the open chamber of his rifle, creating a low, flute-like tone. If a person wasn't attuned to it, they could mistake it for a natural forest sound.

After hearing Evelyn's story, a recent episode made more sense to Donna. A man had come for her in the late afternoon for his wife's delivery way up the creek. It was a tidy home, with a fresh coat of white calcimite on the newspapered walls. The delivery was normal, but Donna wasn't finished bathing the healthy baby and mother until way past dark.

"Take some nourishment with us," the mother offered, "Emaline is stirring up some hogs and hominy." Donna gladly accepted a bowl of hominy and chunks of ham with gravy. Rather than spend the night with them, she decided to ride back to the outpost. The husband said he'd walk along a piece. Considering the night and the steep trail, this comforted Donna. She noticed that he checked the chamber on his rifle and slipped it under his long coat.

Several times she heard tapping sounds from above the trail. It must have been a similar form of local "telephone." When they reached the drainage that would take her the rest of the way to the center, she told the man she was comfortable going alone the rest of the way.

"All right, Miss Donna. No need to be uneasy o' the rest o' the trail."

At the time, she was pleased that the man had been so courteous to accompany her half way back to the outpost. After hearing Evelyn's story, she realized that it must have been moonshine country. He accompanied her for her safety, more than a simple courtesy.

Evelyn's Night Out

*E*velyn's day started out normally, as normal as a day in the FNS could be. She and Ginger were working at Brutus clinic on Bullskin Creek. After treating walk-ins for the day, they sat down to fill in the day's records and plan their next on-district horseback circuit. Ham and potatoes were warming for their dinner. The housekeeper had done the evening milking and was leaving.

A young boy appeared with news that his sister had stubbed her foot on a rough plank, and gotten a huge splinter. The nurses knew the family; the mother was registered and expecting a baby soon. The father was away from home, floating a log raft downriver to the mill. The boy was the only other one home besides his mother, who'd made a wise decision to send him for help rather than bring the injured girl to the center herself.

"Seein' that plug o' wood in Lissy's foot kinda makes me feel jiggly," he said.

The nurses could imagine.

"Mommy made Lissy to lie down, and she gave her a cup o' Daddy's mule," he said, meaning "white mule" or moonshine.

Evelyn told Ginger she would ride out to take care of the girl, pleased for an escape from the drudgery of an evening spent record-keeping. "I'd rather go than sit inside on a beautiful evening," she thought. "No need for both of us," she said to Ginger. "Sounds like I can take care of it," she declared with her customary self-confidence. She grabbed her nurse's kit, and while she saddled up, the housekeeper packed a ham sandwich and thermos of coffee for her to take. The home was at the outskirts of their known district. There wasn't enough daylight to make it there and back, allowing time for the care of the girl. Evelyn made sure her flashlight worked and returned it to her bag. "Sammy," she said, "you can ride with me on Rusty, okay?" Ginger helped the boy onto the horse. Evelyn called for her dog Panda to wake up and join them. She swung up onto the saddle behind the boy. "if I'm not back an hour after dark, call the mounties," she said cavalierly, and rode away. The delighted boy flashed Ginger a gap-toothed grin, his legs dangling awkwardly.

Evelyn arrived at the home and like the boy said, Alissa had a serious splinter in her foot. She was in bed lying on her back, her foot on a rolled-up quilt. In an unfocused way, the girl watched the nurse wash her hands and sterilize tweezers and other shiny instruments. "That was good that you elevated Lissy's foot," Evelyn commented. She said nothing about the improvised "tranquilizer." Heaven only knew how potent the homemade spirits were, but it probably soothed the girl's anxiety and there would be no need for any more of the stuff.

"Let's see about getting this piece of kindling out of your foot," Evelyn said. Folks were charmed by the dark-haired nurse. They knew she really cared about them. Sometimes her fearlessness got her in a bit of trouble, and her blue eyes sparkled when she told one of those stories. Laying her hand on Alissa's forehead, she said, "You'll be skipping rope before you know it, Sweetie." The flesh around the splinter had swelled, making the jagged wood hard to remove, but eventually Evelyn was able to get all the fragments out. She cleaned and loosely bandaged the wound.

"You need to keep that foot elevated, and no unnecessary walking for a couple of days until I come back to check on you, Lissy," she said, adding with a wink, "No dancing for awhile, okay, Twinkletoes?"

Alissa giggled.

Evelyn told the mother to check it every hour and be sure to send Sammy back down to the center with news if red streaks appeared, or if Lissy became fevered. "She's a brave girl," the nurse said. "Now that she's mending she won't need any more 'mule.' You may give her these aspirins every four hours for pain."

Evelyn was eager to be on her way and use what light was left in the shallow arc of sky above the trees. With her pleasing grin, she said goodbye to the three of them. She decided to take a shortcut on a less-used trail to another creek that would get her to Bullskin, and back down to the center. The pleasant night sky had become a little less friendly. The wind began stirring the trees.

She went against FNS policy and deviated from where she had told Ginger she would be going. Panda circled a few times, reluctant to follow. Evelyn kept riding, thinking she should reach the drainage any moment. "We can always turn back if things don't work out soon, Panda," she said.

It was now too dark to make out landmarks, like the grove of poplars. Evelyn started to doubt the direction she was headed, but the longer she rode, the less inclined she was to turn back. She saw an opening just wide enough for her horse in the dense woods on her right, and turned onto the overgrown trail. It seemed to be going downhill, and would probably take her to a drainage. The wind was gusting and the trees seemed outraged by being disturbed from the peace of the evening.

She came into a small clearing, straining her eyes to see in the dark. She could make out a building on her left, probably a barn, and beyond, maybe a cabin showing no light.

A man's voice shot out of the dark: "You! Hold it right thar!"

Her horse stopped and arched his neck, his ears swiveled forward. Startled, Evelyn held her breath; her pulse pounded in her ears. Panda barked protectively until Evelyn was able to shush him.

"Hello-o-o . . . I'm with the Frontier Nurses!"

He approached silently, the wind overpowering any sound his footsteps would have made. He kept his rifle lowered at his side. He came close enough to see for himself she was what she said. "You alone?"

"Yes sir." She immediately regretted her answer. "No sir . . . I have a dog."

Y'er from Brutus, I s'pect," he said, "and if you want to get there tonight you'd best go back a differ'nt way than the way y'er headed."

"I expect to do that, sir."

"They's a better path if you turn around, and at the edge of the clearing, turn up the hill a ways, till you find the trail on yer left. You'll reach the branch that'll take you back down to Bullskin. No one ortent beast you if you stay on the trail."

"Yes, sir. I am expected back at the center now," she said.

"You jest head right on out o' here thataway," he said, and he backed away in the direction of the cabin, his face fixed on her until the night seemed to swallow him whole.

She turned around and started back to the edge of his clearing, her heart racing and her thoughts sluggish as the rain started pelting her wool cap and shoulders. She'd not thought of the weather when she left her center, and realized she had not brought her slicker. "Okay Rusty, let's get ourselves out of here and think our situation through."

She turned the horse back the way she thought she'd come, and rode a few steps. She stopped and watched for signs of where the man had gone. There still was no light in the cabin. Panda, jealously protecting his master, darted from side to side, but in close proximity to her horse.

She was so muddled, she nudged the horse forward into the agitated blackness of the forest and rode for what she figured was a quarter mile, but had no idea where she was. She stopped, reached behind her, and felt into her left saddlebag for her flashlight. Snapping it on, she checked her watch. It was 9:30, the time she really should have been riding back into the cozy barn at the Brutus Center. How she wished that was exactly what she was doing right now!

"I can't dwell on wishes, I need to solve our problem, Rusty," she said, stroking the horse's neck. The man's warning words ran through her head. "I've got an idea. Let's ride back to that man's barn. It's far enough from his cabin, I think we'd be better off there. As soon as it's light, mark my words, we'll high-tail it back home!"

She turned the horse around. "Come on Panda . . . " There was no sign of the dog.

"*Panda!*"

The dog had disappeared. Evelyn had no idea which way he'd gone, but she knew better than continue to call him. She retraced her steps back to the clearing and approached the sulking barn. In her desperation it looked almost welcoming. The hard rain had let up, but the wind was still gusting. She tied her horse under the eaves of the barn, and loosened the cinch but left the saddle on. "There you go, Rusty, your saddle will help keep you dry." She deliberated a moment, then in spite of the discomfort it meant for her horse, decided to leave his bridle on as well, in case she needed to ride away in a hurry. She slipped inside the building and sat up against the wall closest to the door. She gripped her flashlight and hunkered down, wishing she had her slicker over her for warmth. She was not sorry the dog had bolted. Even a harmless barn mouse would have caused him to bark, calling attention to the unwelcome guests.

Ginger didn't know what to think when Panda trotted back to the center alone. Evelyn had said she'd be home an hour after dark. It was way past that now. Why would the dog have returned without the woman and her horse? Ginger knew better than to start off up the creek herself to try to find Evelyn. She decided to call the only center with a phone into Wendover to get a message to Ellery to see if he had any ideas about what she should do. He knew the country. Maybe he could put her mind at ease.

"It was a simple injury up Bullskin," Ginger said into the phone, trying to force her voice through the wires without sounding desperate, "but she said she'd be back by now. Her dog just showed up here." After she hung up, she regretted having made the call. Evelyn was probably fine. She must have changed her stated plan and decided to stay the night with the family; or had decided to see one of their pre-natals, and was staying with that family. Especially since the weather had turned sour. Surely the family insisted she stay over. Surely Evelyn was fine.

But why did the dog return alone . . . ?

Half an hour later, Ellery rang her up to say he could drive a Jeep as far as her center, then saddle up Ginger's horse and try to locate Evelyn.

But Mrs. Breckinridge caught wind of the trouble and in a rare instance of using the Wendover telephone herself, firmly told Ginger that she did not want two good people out in such a night, and to let things shake out as they would. "Evelyn is resourceful and determined, and is probably taking the night somewhere along the trail," she said. "We have enough friends in the mountains that she is probably being looked after with the highest kindness," she concluded, hanging up the hissing telephone line.

Now the entire communication chain knew about Evelyn's truancy by deviating from her stated plan; and of Ginger's panic in her attempt to get help.

Ginger couldn't shake her uneasiness. Evelyn was known for her optimism, curiosity, and trustfulness. Although the nurses had many friends in the area, it was dangerous country. There were always physical risks to a lone horseback rider. And how could she have gotten separated from the dog? "Oh why didn't I go with her," Ginger scolded herself over and over.

She spent a miserable night, worrying about the pretty young nurse.

"I was so stupid to think there might be a better way out," Evelyn realized. "Of course the boy came the shortest way to get help." Thoughts like that circled in her mind all the long night.

The wind moaned through the drafty building.

"And what that man said about no one ought to 'beast' me? I've only heard that term used about hornets coming around to 'beast the livestock'. . . he wasn't talking about hornets . . . how foolish I've been!"

She put two fingers over the lens of her flashlight, switched it on, and cautiously shined it around her. With the light partly shrouded, she spotted a pitchfork against the wall, retrieved it and laid it across her lap. She hadn't eaten since noon but had no appetite for the sandwich or coffee in her saddlebag. She tried to shut her ears to sounds outside the barn long enough to rest her mind.

"Maybe it's unfair to make Rusty stand outside in his saddle and bridle all night . . . " As she rose to tend the horse, a loose piece of tin patch rattled sharply near the door, vibrating in the wind. She caught her breath and froze for a moment, then rationalized, " . . . he needs to stay where he is, to be ready for a quick escape."

What would she do if something *did* alarm her to an escape? She had no idea which way to ride. Only oncoming daylight would help usher her out of there.

Evelyn rode into Brutus center an hour after sunrise, cold, exhausted, and humbled. Ginger hugged her and cried with relief. Evelyn bent down and vigorously petted Panda. "This dog has more sense than I have!" she exclaimed. "Dear, I'll take care of the clinic for the morning," Ginger told her. "You get yourself some hot water, wash up, eat a hot breakfast, and rest a few hours."

"I can't think of anything I'd rather do," Evelyn said, dropping her wet baggage on the linoleum and slogging into her room to change out of her wet clothes.

"Did you hear about Evelyn's night out?" The nurses blurted when Donna next joined them at Hyden. "She left out of Brutus for a simple house call, and got lost trying to find a shortcut back. A storm came and she had to spend the night in an unfriendly stranger's barn way up Hackberry Branch!"

"She was headed way off into Owsley!" added another.

"Oh dear! Thank goodness she made it back safely!" Donna exclaimed. "I bet she's not inclined to go wandering alone outside of the district again," she added to herself.

A Mule Named Tenacity

"She's tough as whang leather, but she's an easy keeper
and she's been growed up to work."
"You talkin' about Hutchin's woman or his mule?"

— overheard conversation, Hyden, Kentucky

"Cross a good mare with a jack donkey and she can throw you a right smart animal," Ellery explained to Donna as he removed the mule's harness. "They get their mammy and their pappy's best traits bred in 'em." Donna liked to catch Ellery when he was between tasks. Gentle and modest, once he was at ease with her, he willingly shared his homespun wisdom.

Ellery changed the subject long enough to tell her he'd been thinking of apples as a cash crop. "O' course, it's a long-time away idea," he added.

"If I had to choose only one fruit in the whole world, it would be the apple," Donna said. The two were standing in front of the Wendover barn. There was a long silence, but neither of them felt awkward. The sun had dropped behind the ridge and the evening sky couldn't decide between gold or purple. A sprinkle of bats fluttered from the rafters and passed right over their heads. The mule lowered his head slightly as Ellery slid the headstall over his long ears. Again, Donna was impressed by his gentle, strong hands.

"You know, fer a mule to be borned takes two weeks longer than fer a horse colt. It takes that long fer t' grow their ears!" They both chuckled at the old joke. "A mule will go a lot longer on a lot less than a horse. They won't frash theirselves like a tempery horse neither," he added. "It took me some long talkin' before Miz Breckinridge made the choice to buy a couple o' mules at first. She was pretty set on those brought-on horses."

There's not a lot of panache surrounding mules; they don't conjure up ideas about the good life like a smartly-dressed rider, head up and heels down atop a well-bred horse. Mules are linked with hard work and a low life. Who hasn't heard the well-worn expression, "stubborn as a mule"?

The FNS used mules for the farm work on its acreage at Wendover. To be self-reliant, the compound had five acres along the river planted in corn and vegetables. The mules soon proved their worthiness. Plowing was their main occupation, but they were also very useful for moving heavy objects during clearing and building projects, or skidding up logs and large debris left over after the rivers subsided from the tides. If a vehicle got stuck in some sink-hole, the easiest way to solve the problem was to harness a mule and pull the helpless contraption to solid ground.

"Not long after we got this here mule, there was a big tide. Once't the water went back down, I harnessed him to go get a mess o' logs off'n beside the Middle Fork. Them logs was jack-strawed ever' which way, so's I couldn't tell which one was first. Finally I just grappled what I could and let the mule straighten 'em out as they skid up that grade," Ellery said with obvious pride in his voice. "When Miz Breckinridge saw that mule pullin' that mess o' firewood all the way up to her place, she decided to name him 'Tenacity.' He never even broke a sweat."

Donna loved to hear Ellery's stories. His chest seemed to swell as deep as it was broad. It reminded her of her dad, also a modest man with wholesome, quiet pride.

Tenacity the mule with courier
— *Reid family photo.*

It was district day for Donna and Evelyn at Beech Fork nursing center. They would be making home visits by way of an eight- or ten-mile circuit out of the nursing center. Ellery had asked Susan, a young courier, to ride Tenacity from Wendover to the Beech Fork outpost for him. He would drive the half-ton truck over the next day, and harness the mule to skid downed timber out to stockpile firewood for the upcoming winter. As the nurses prepared for their rounds, Susan asked the nurses if she could ride along on Tenacity. They were happy to have her company. Donna remembered Ellery's comments about mules. As Susan prepared to mount, Donna was confident that even though this mule was the oldest in the Service, the animal's bred-in stamina and sure-footedness would bring Susan back home safely.

The November day was gray and chilly; the naked trees rattled in the occasional gust of wind. The three riders left the roadway and made their way single file up the narrow trail. Autumn daylight was scarce in the hollows but the young women were in bright spirits, chatting constantly. When the talk slowed, Donna's thoughts turned to Ellery, and the comfort of his companionship. It pleased her that he was coming to her center in the morning. It gave her something to look forward to. She began to imagine his strong, gentle arms around her. These moments were a vacation from her many responsibilities.

Her musing ended as they pulled up to their first visit. They'd been called to treat an axe injury that had happened earlier that morning. As the nurses cleansed and sutured the man's leg, he seemed to be struggling with a different kind of problem. Sensing this, keeping her eyes on her bandaging task, Donna asked him if there might be something else they could do while they were there. Yes, he finally admitted, "I'm not moved to disfurnish you ladies, but could my boy use yer mule to skid the trees I cut 'afore I pinked my leg? We mought o' been able to manage our own selves with a peavey and a winch, but since I'm laid up in this way, it would be favorable to use the mule."

Of course they consented.

His wife said, "You'uns will be stayin' over fer some lunch, then. I'll knock a tater in the haid and warm up some gravy." She boiled water for elm bark tea as they finished the meal.

When the boy returned, Tenacity had worked up a sweat in spite of the cold air. They let him cool off some before continuing on their rounds.

They made one post-partum visit and while the nurses examined the mother, Susan was delighted to help bathe and dry the baby. They stayed a little longer than usual so Susan could hold the newborn awhile. At the next home a child presented an ear infection; farther on they used antibiotic salve to treat a child who had developed impetigo from an infected chigger bite. It was suppertime, so they lingered long enough to eat their sandwiches in the warmth of the family's cabin while three young children watched and giggled bashfully. Before departing, Donna set out her candy bars for them, which awed the children.

It was evening by now; they had already resigned themselves to riding home in the dark.

Not long into their return ride, Evelyn's horse stumbled in a badger hole, nearly unseating her. The horse began favoring the leg, so they dismounted, and by the light of a flashlight wrapped his lower leg from his pastern to his knee the best they could. They decided it would not be wise to add the weight of a rider, so Evelyn rode behind Susan on Tenacity.

Their trail joined the road, and rounding a corner they saw a truck that had slid off the road where it was always shady and had become icy. The nurses recognized Eli and Pete. Using a slab of wood for a makeshift shovel, they were taking turns digging out from under the running board. But the vehicle was still wedged in the ground. The men were very glad to see the horseback nurses, realizing they might be saved the trouble of more digging or a cold walk home in the dark after their long shift at the Lost Creek mine. Wanting to help, the women thought nothing of putting Tenacity's steady strength to another task. Eli produced some rope from the truck bed and looped it around the animal's chest, and slip-knotted it around the front cross frame of the truck. He got in and started the engine. Tenacity knew what needed to be done. Donna stood at his side with his reins in her hand as the mule leaned into the rope. Eli applied some power. The mule pulled, trying to lift the truck out of the deep borrow pit. Tenacity pulled again and again, and out it finally came, to loud engine noise and the whine of a spinning tire. Tenacity stood stock still, but his sides heaved like forge bellows, forcing the hot breath from his flared nostrils. He stepped back to slacken the rope. He swiveled his long ears back and forth, as if awaiting his next orders.

The men removed the makeshift harness, which was all the time Tenacity needed to restore his normal breathing, and the two young women mounted him once more for the last stretch back to Beech Fork.

Susan took care of the animals when they reached the center so the nurses could get started on the day's record-keeping while it was fresh in their minds. Evelyn lit the kerosene lamps and Donna stirred the dawdling fire that the housekeeper had banked before she left for the day. The nurses finished their duties at the oilcloth-covered table, and went to bed.

There were already several folks waiting to be seen in the morning when Ellery stopped in at the center to let them know he was there to do the skidding with Tenacity. "Should be done in short order, as workin' as that mule is," he said. Susan decided to go with Ellery, thinking it would be fun to watch him work with the mule.

Within a few moments, she and Ellery reappeared at the back door. Ellery asked Donna to come outside with them. His face was gray with grief.

"What's the matter?" she asked, as she pulled the door closed behind her.

"Tenacity! He's . . . he's . . . " Susan's voice choked off.

Ellery gently interrupted. "Looks like the old feller rid himself of his earthly labors. He must o' died in his sleep."

"I feel awful!" Susan wailed. "We worked him too hard yesterday! He was *such* a good mule!" She sobbed, and put her head in her hands.

"Like as not, he was jus' plumb wore out," Ellery said, trying to comfort Susan. "You'd not have had any way to know. Hit's better'n him dyin' in a lasty way, of a copperhead bite or losin' his teeth and starvin'." Ellery's kind words settled Susan's distress somewhat. "I misdoubt he suffered any," he added, looking at Donna. In his eyes, she saw his deep sadness, though he remained composed.

Donna put her arm around Susan; Ellery stood, his gaze dropping toward his boots, his worn hat in his hands. Donna realized she'd never seen him without his fedora. His dark hair was full and youthful, with a permanent bend where the hat brim rested just above his ears. She wanted to hug and hold him and feel his strong chest. After a respectful pause, he put his hat back on. "Now you get over your glaum, young lady," he told Susan. "You're needed back at Wendover." Discreetly removing a shovel from his truck, he added, "Take the truck there and tell 'em that the ol' mule 'spired o' old age, and I'll catch a ride after takin' proper care of him." To Donna he quietly added that he'd have to "round up a couple o' local men to help bury the critter."

During a break in her duties, Donna's thoughts came back around to the morning's sad happening, and the notion that Tenacity the mule was a lot like the people she served – folks living in a forgotten frontier in hand-built dwellings in the pretty clearings; the hand-dug wells, hand-made furniture, and no hardware store nearby. Was it only stubborn people who chose to live long on this hard-yielding land? But stubborn people had a set-jaw way about them, and these people weren't like that. They were kind and gracious. Like Ellery. When facing a job, there was no hesitating. A quiet strength came forth with no complaints. Donna could identify with these descendants of stalwart English, Welsh and Scots-Irish settlers. She had come to love Kentucky's mountain people. "Tenacity the mule was a lot like them," she thought. When blown by gusts of adversity they would rather break than bend.

As she returned to her tasks, she understood these folks had held on to something that people from beyond the mountains had given up among the aisles of their department stores in their hunt for the switched-on easy life – a spirit that fades among the sidewalks and streetlights, and is lost forever.

Coal Boom

"At noon, men broke out their lunch boxes and the man I was with, a miner for 35 years, spread two or three thick sandwiches, a raw onion and a piece of pie on his lap. When he ate his pie first, I wondered why. 'Cause,' he said simply but eloquently, 'the roof might fall.'"

— *"Joe Creasy's Kentucky,"* published in the *Louisville Courier-Journal*

War has a mighty appetite, especially a World War. In addition to men and women, it craves fuel, steel, aluminum, building materials, food, communications equipment, chemicals and textiles. Not one of these things gets from where it starts to where it's needed without some form of mineral to transport it or forge it into something useful from within red-hot furnaces.

Aluminum becomes aircraft skin only after bauxite is mined out of the ground; then hauled, crushed and heated throughout several processes. Steel for tanks, ships and artillery must be wrested from iron ore that has been mined and shipped to a foundry. The monster foundry furnaces hulking throughout the nation's industrial states gobbled up coal twenty-four hours a day. Electric light to illuminate factories where military uniforms were sewn together came from coal-burning generating plants. Locomotives burned coal getting coal trains to the factories.

The nation depended on Kentucky's bituminous coal to keep its furnaces fed and its factory lights on. It was Kentucky's patriotic duty to fuel the Allies' ability to vanquish the dual threat of Nazi Germany and the Japanese Empire.

Mine owners whipped the flanks of their production lines, squeezing maximum effort out of their men and machines. The volume of coal hauled out of Kentucky doubled, then tripled, from pre-war times. The coal boom was not only patriotic, but very profitable.

For the mine owners.

The high cost was borne by dust-blackened miners. Longer hours on the exhausting and tedious job, and a six-day work week, pushed the men and machines nearly to the breaking point. Fatigue led to carelessness. In their haste, miners took safety short-cuts. They had to resort to makeshift supplies, like defective fuse material that could blow early. When the sawmills couldn't keep up, miners skimped on the placement of supporting mine timbers. They drove overloaded trucks faster on the twisty, narrow haul roads. Safety training for men coming on the job was given short shrift. They skipped maintenance on exhaust fans that removed poison gas and combustible coal dust from the work area. The foul mix of deep earth gas and atomized coal dust was an incendiary fuel that exploded with a tiny spark.

In the midst of the war years, the *Hazard Herald* reported that "nearly forty percent of state accidents occur in coal mines." The report was based on official Industrial Relations Commission statistics. It was not unusual for a dozen or more men to lose their lives in Kentucky mines each month.[5]

On December 26, 1945, the slow dawn began to light up a typical winter day along Straight Creek, just over the line in Clay County. The slumbering land lay under a thin blanket of snow around Vern and Sarah's little house. The dormant trees stood motionless in the still air. Even the creek was silent, ice-locked until spring's thaw. Sarah had been up a while, making bread and soaking beans for Vern's meal when he returned from his shift. Their four children were in the room they shared, playing quietly on this after-Christmas morning.

About eight o'clock, the ground was shaken by a deep "THUMP-UMP" followed by smoke coming from the narrow opening of a mine. Sarah and everyone else who heard it knew instantly there had been an explosion in the Straight Creek mine.

---

[5] In adjacent Harlan County, a memorial was erected at the courthouse in 2009 with the names of the miners who lost their lives in the mines in Harlan County between 1912 and 2000. Harlan is one of Kentucky's 120 counties, with an area of only 467 square miles, about one quarter the size of Rhode Island. It lists over 1,200 names.

Sarah had been too young to understand when, twenty-eight years before, the worst disaster in Kentucky's coal mining history killed sixty-two men in western Kentucky. The local people didn't know those miners personally, but they felt the loss. There had been other disasters closer to home, cave-ins and explosions killing and maiming several men at a time. Grown-ups hushed their recollections of mining horrors around young ears, but children of mining families couldn't help but absorb the edgy air of trepidation.

Mining families never rest completely free of the worry that comes when the family bread-winner and children's father takes his dinner bucket and disappears a thousand feet below the surface to intrude into the earth's secret places undisturbed since deep time. Sarah hid from their children the fact that she hated that Vern worked there. "What good would it be if he felt our five fraught-out souls clingin' to him ever' time he left the house fer work?" she conceded, recognizing they had no other prospects.

Now a deadly accident threatened Vern and all the husbands, sons and fathers, and the families were helpless to stop the billowing smoke and catastrophe below.

Fire killed several of the men immediately. The rest scurried to gather their lunch buckets, drinkable water, and try to find a safe place where the black damp – deadly carbon monoxide mixed with coal dust – wouldn't kill them before rescuers dug their way through the collapsed earth to get them out. The explosion created enough of a quake that underground springs released water into their chamber. A cold, black pool was slowly rising around the miners.

Two days and two nights passed as rescuers located scattered bodies and tunneled their way to the survivors. In her gut, Sarah felt the worsening odds of her husband being alive, but she kept hope in her heart. They brought up the nine survivors they found, and Vern was not among them. The newspaper in Middlesboro reported daily on the unfolding rescue, and listed each lost miner's name, age, and how many children he had. Seeing Vern's name in newspaper type ripped the hope from her heart. She turned her thoughts to protecting and providing for her children.

The final death toll was thirty-one men, leaving at least eighty-five fatherless children.

"It's somethin' you never ferget," Sarah explained. "The papers get it over with and go on to other news, and people go on livin' but miners carry the loss inside 'em like a vigil."

News of the tragedy hit the FNS staff like a lightning bolt. The nurses were accustomed to the dreadful slate fall injuries, haul truck accidents on the steep roads, eye injuries or burns and fingers blown off from explosives. They were dismayed at the cases of black-lung disease, and the run-down condition of some of the miners, who were very susceptible to tuberculosis. But an underground explosion ruined many lives at once – either with quick death from the blast, tortuous death from the fire, the lung-searing toxic gas, or suffocation from lack of oxygen. Trapped men who survived languished in the tunnels, blocked from salvation until rescuers mustered and began the urgent but puzzling task of locating them and digging them out. Rescuers have reported seeing arrows scrawled on tunnel walls to guide them to survivors. During the Straight Creek mine rescue, one rescuer found a miner's body, still in a kneeling position near a sign he'd written out on a piece of slate:

"God bless us all is my prayer."

More than three hundred men took part in the rescue, coming from all directions and several counties.

"If ever you find yerself trapped in a mine, you'll want another miner comin' after you," one bystander said. There was a strong brotherhood among miners, and the determined rescue crew was buffeted back repeatedly by fires and the presence of white damp – methane gas. The deadly barrier held off the rescuers from retrieving all of the bodies, some feared to be more than twelve hundred feet in. By January, twenty unaccounted-for men were given up for lost and the mine was sealed, entombing them. Sarah had to wait three more years, when the mine was excavated, before her husband's body was brought out.

"It's hard to pay proper respects to your man and your children's daddy when you don't know where he is," Sarah said as Vern's remains were retrieved in the final rescue. "We were much pleased he was finally able to be brought to a proper resting place."

The kind men kept from her the fact that all they recognized of her husband were his scorched overalls and his good teeth.

"I can't believe there are men who are willing to work in the mines, with such bad conditions, no matter the pay!" cried Evelyn after the news made its way to Wendover. She and a courier were waiting in front of the barn, where Ellery was just finishing rasping the sharp shoe nail points off Rusty's hooves. "I treated one man who told me he worked every day shoveling coal his whole shift. He could hardly stand up straight. In truth, he's broken without any fractures. Our hospitals are filling with cases of black-lung . . . don't they think of their wives and children? "

Ellery turned from his work and paused a moment as if to let the bitterness of her question dissolve in the air. In his kind, laconic way he tried to explain. "Miz Evelyn, they's not a lot o' other ways t' support their families. And back o' that, minin'-folk are ever staunch to the habit o' minin'."

"But why don't they demand that the mine owners keep the mines safe? How can people just stand by during all this tragedy?" she asked in exasperation.

"It's noble work," he stated. "They know the odds are against 'em. Miners is grateful doin' what they do ever' day they live beyond their shift."

Floating the Tides

"It didn't look like dangerous work, them logs just afloatin' nice and restful . . .
Until the river riled 'em up and sent thousand-pound lunkers all to once, all
decided on ragin' agin' one another."

— A logger's comments about the springtime log float

Donna was working at the Hyden hospital. It was an adjustment to be back among the most serious cases needing in-patient care, like Herbert, an aged lumberman whom Donna had first treated some time ago on district. She remembered him as tough-skinned and independent, and at first he refused when she referred him to the hospital for cancer treatment.

"I don't aim to leave my home and kin to rot in a strange place like a goose egg in the sun," he had argued. But when there was nothing more his family could do at home to keep him comfortable, and he understood that his wife would be welcome to visit him, he relented. By then he was too weak to put up much of a fight. His wife came to see him in spite of the difficulty of getting to the Hyden hospital from their place a dozen miles away. The unspoken, larger snag was the realization that for the first time in his adult life, Herbert was no longer in control. He couldn't bring this illness down like felling a stubborn oak tree. It was hard for her to watch him waste away from the strapping man he had been.

Herbert reminded Donna of folks she knew back home, loggers who took pride working in the hardwood maple forests. She enjoyed asking him about his work in the woods. She liked his stories, visualizing him in his full vigor, even though each day the cancer wore him down like a dull cross-cut saw.

One morning he awoke and, sitting up against the bedstead, surprised the nurses by singing a verse of Stephen Foster's song, "Hard Times Come Again No More." His voice wasn't strong, but he sang with feeling:

While we seek mirth and beauty
and music light and gay
there are frail ones fainting at the door.
Though their voices are silent
their pleading looks will say
oh, hard times come again no more.

The nurses gathered around and clapped.

Once he caught his breath, he asked them, "Did you know that Stephen Foster died drunk, at half my age, with only thirty-seven cents to his name? After all the music he gave us!" His eyes shone as he started singing "My Old Kentucky Home." Everyone within earshot joined in:

The sun shines bright in the old Kentucky home,
'Tis summer, the darkies[6] are gay,
The corn top's ripe and the meadow's in bloom
While the birds make music all the day.
The young folks roll on the little cabin floor,
All merry, all happy, and bright;
By 'n' by hard times comes a' knocking at the door,
Then my old Kentucky home . . .

He drifted from the lyrics as the others sang on. He joined in again with,

Weep no more, my lady,
Oh weep no more today!
We will sing one song for the old Kentucky home,
For the old Kentucky home far away . . .

Exhausted, his eyes closed and he fell asleep. The nurses and others who had gathered stood a moment together, moved by his passion, then drifted back to their duties.

---

[6] "My Old Kentucky Home" became the official state song in 1928. The term "darkies" was replaced with "people" by an act of the Kentucky legislature in 1986. Foster's lyrics usually revealed his abhorrence to slavery and the breakup of slave families.

On Donna's rare afternoons off from the hospital, she would ride Jefferson or catch a car ride with a courier or nurse to Wendover. She would check on her Burt Lake tomatoes and watermelon plants, hoping that Ellery would be there. He always made time to visit with her.

Sure enough, his old pickup was parked below the barn. As she got out of the Jeep, he spotted her walking to the garden and waved. He set his tools down and ambled over to join her. While Donna pulled a few weeds, they chatted about little things.

Ellery then began talking of bigger things. He'd been thinking about the future, and knew shoeing horses would be hard to do in his old age. "Most o' my labors take place no higher'n a horse's knee," he said.

"I'll say," Donna agreed. "I don't know of many old horseshoers without back problems." A person's health was always on her mind – she felt a pang of concern for Ellery's.

He waited a bit, watching her pull weeds, then went on to explain that he also wanted something of his own, and had been thinking again about the notion of his own apple orchard.

"I miss the apple trees we have up home," Donna said.

"I know of a piece of land with good sunlight and drainage," Ellery added, "and with no family to support as of this time . . . "

Donna felt her face get warm, and she turned away from him, pretending to find some important weeds that needed pulling.

After another pause, he went on to explain that his apple crop could become profitable as he stepped back from full-time blacksmithing. "I begun thinkin' o' someone to start learnin' the job by me. Natch'erly, it'll take a while fer to learn all that goes on around here, being sprawled out so."

She straightened up and said her tomatoes were "nearly ready for their taste test, and how about those little watermelons coming on . . . "

Right then, they were interrupted by the comical honk of the Jeep's horn. It was Donna's ride. She was more comfortable with the conversation ended, but to Ellery it was an annoyance to be interrupted such. The two said good-bye, but only after Ellery took a step toward Donna, as if to hug her, but stopped.

As she got in the Jeep next to the courier she hoped her warm face didn't reveal her attraction to Ellery. On the ride back to the hospital Donna began to understand that Ellery was trusting her with his dream. She appreciated that he was pondering the idea of including her in his future plans. "I am so slow to catch on," she said to herself. "I wonder why he's not a family man already." It was not the first time this question had occurred to her. He was very attractive, in a rustic, capable way. She had no doubt that Ellery would have his orchard, and in a few years would see a nice apple crop. "I wish I hadn't gotten so flustered. I hope I didn't hurt his feelings," she thought. His kind, steady manner was as winsome as leather you'd just worked over with neatsfoot oil. "He could build a fire in a downpour," she mused. "I know Dad would approve." Her father had quipped to his girls to "find a man who's a good shot and who can build a fire in a downpour, and you'll never go hungry."

Her thoughts abruptly broke off when they arrived in the whirl of activity at the hospital. A man on a hand-made stretcher was being pulled from the back of the FNS station wagon. "Scalding accident!" someone hollered. "Stave mill boiler blew!"

The injured man had been working next to the boiler at the barrel stave mill when it exploded, spewing super-heated water. His co-workers threw together a stretcher and, to save many miles, they hauled him to the river, loaded him on a small boat and floated him down the Middle Fork where the FNS car could meet him at Hyden for the trip to the hospital up Thousandsticks.

Donna had no time to mull over Ellery's comments, or his intentions at the garden. That would have to wait until this new emergency got handled.

Lumber was a very important part of the economy. Like mining, it was a dangerous way to make a living from one end of the industry to the other. There were so many ways life in the woods turned deadly. Timber being cut or hauled followed convoluted laws of gravity. As your saw made the final few strokes, a falling giant could split and "barber chair" on you, levering up a deadly shank of raw wood that could gut you like a fish. Cut timber could get hung up on a neighbor tree, and fall when you least expected it. No wonder these hangers were called "widow makers." Swinging a double-bitted axe at resilient limbs, while walking along a felled tree, required perfect balance. A misstep could alter your aim. Shins sometimes got in the way of the axe.

Men harnessed horses, oxen or mules to skid the logs to a place where the spring tides could lift and carry them downstream to the sawmill. Men mangled their hands if their animal spooked or if the log rolled while they were chaining it up or releasing it.

The collection of downed logs made quite a raft when they started floating. Men had to shepherd them, lashing a few together to provide a bit of organization but the rest were at the mercy of the rushing waters. Men in spiked – "caulked" or "corked" – logging boots would leap from log to log, using a heavy peavey pole to wrangle jammed logs. Riding the flotilla was the easiest way to move the logs, but was more dangerous than bull-riding.

Men handling sawmill blade — *FNS photo, courtesy of Univ. of Kentucky archives.*

Then came the milling process. The sawmills were crude collections of spinning saw blades and conveyor chains. Some were powered by primitive boilers with no safety valves. All of them were fire hazards, with sawdust accumulating beneath the friction-hot machinery. If your mind wasn't clearly focused one hundred-and-ten percent, you might look down and see where your hand used to be.

Now a horrible accident threatened the life of a man who supported his family by working beside a faulty boiler trying to bend oak into barrel staves.

 ⌒ ⌒

To help out one of the Hyden nurses, on her day off Donna offered to make a home visit. There were young children who hadn't come to the clinic for their booster shots. The mother welcomed Donna, glad for the company, and for the nurse's compassionate ear.

"A man takes anything and ever'thing that comes along fer a little cash to provide fer his young'uns," the woman began explaining to Donna, who knew she'd just lost her husband, Conrad.

"Would you like to tell me about it?"

"The last I see'd of Con'erd, he was sittin' right thar on the porch." She paused and smiled. "He had on his best wool socks and he sat right thar, lacin' up his tall corked boots." She described how he rubbed hog grease into them to keep the river water from soaking his feet, at least for awhile.

The man left the house that morning to help float the log raft down the river.

"He fell off'n his log, and could o' took a hit on the head. He couldn't make his way back onto the raft. Them logs had him trapped. They's no way to stop the raft, so one of the men got hisself over t' the river bank and looked around but it was no use. Con'erd was gone."

They never found his body. No one needed to inform her that after the water went down, a tell-tale piece of his shirt was discovered way downstream, hanging grimly from an overhanging tree branch. The plaid flannel was ragged, and was the only clue they needed to close their minds on the idea that the turbulence and heavy logs had mangled him. It would have been impossible to know how far downstream his body traveled in that torrent.

"The river swallowed him whole, and never thought it fit to give him back up," the widow said. "My wakin' side told me he was never comin' back, but my dreamin' side sees him back home ever'day, sittin' right thar on that porch, takin' off his boots."

Donna put her hand on the woman's arm.

"It's like that when they ain't no body to properly bury," the widow said in a resigned tone. "They ain't nothing to set a proper gravestone over, so the spirit of the departed is ever restless. I s'pose I'll keep a'dreamin' that as long as the good Lord lets me live."

When old Herbert heard of the young logger losing his life in the tides, he talked it over with Donna. He wanted to understand Conrad's death. They figured he had either been knocked unconscious and drowned or had become hypothermic and died with little suffering.

Herbert recognized the irony of outliving all the risks of a lifetime of battling giant timber, only to succumb to cancer. He envied the young man's death. "If I could o' chosen a way to go, I believe I may have preferred that kind of passing instead of this slow turnin' inside out," he told Donna. "But then, I'd o' missed these last many days," he added, patting the nurse's hand.

The day came for his wife to be with him for the final vigil. "When you get one of these tough Kentucky men corralled so you can see 'em up close, they're not so crusty," she said to Donna. "He always smelled of fresh-cut timber. Kind of a warm, sap smell."

Donna replied that she understood.

The woman fixed her aged eyes on the nurse. "He was at peace here among you folks. I never knew him to be so thoughty."

Once that tough shell broke away, you found their gentle souls, Donna thought. She was glad to have known and treated Herbert. He was a fine man. This country was full of fine men like Herbert and Conrad. Like Ellery.

She felt a strange combination of sorrow and anticipation. She was deeply saddened to think this woman would never again feel her husband's protective arms around her. Donna was young and had so much love and life in front of her.

High Water Mark

"There is something peculiarly cruel about a flash flood because there is so little time. That is why many people lost their cows and chickens as well as their household possessions . . . If people ran fast enough they were able to get out of their homes, but were able to take nothing with them except the babies."

— Mary Breckinridge, FNS *Quarterly Bulletin*,
Summer 1947

The nurses heard the rain peppering the roof when they went to bed. As unyielding as it seemed that particular night, hard rain is normal in June. Rain, shine, sleet or worse, on district days, the nurses were expected to get up early and prepare to leave for however long it might take to complete their circuit. They treated everything from jaundiced newborns to the aged, who finally would push aside their diffidence and admit to having a carbuncle on their backside.

After breakfast, Francis, the junior nurse, went outside to check out the unusual sound of the little creek that ran below their quarters. She hurried back in. "Come listen!" she blurted. "The creek sounds like the mighty waters of Niagara!" Mother Nature had been holding her breath since 1930, when a drought had starved out many farmers of the southeast states. Now, in June 1947, with a mighty exhale, heavy rain broke loose, and didn't let up for weeks.

Donna changed into her rubber boots and she and Francis put on their FNS hooded slickers, loading last-minute supplies into the Jeep. Heading down the river road, they got as far as the swinging bridge at Owl's Nest. They stopped and stared in awe as it began to break apart in the rushing torrent gagging with lumber, barrel staves and furniture. The folks from the tidy white house across the river were frantically loading their belongings into a small boat to cross the swelling water and move the bulky load to higher ground. Their orderly vegetable garden and flower patch were already gone, and the dirty water was heaving itself against the upstream side of the house, threatening its footings.

The nurses intended to continue, but not far from that spectacle a landslide blocked their way. They decided to drive to Hyden. It was a chaotic scene there, with people trying to lead horses and cows to safe ground, some were going about in boats or canoes, and a few were wallowing slowly through the high water in cars and trucks. The river was muddy brown, carrying trees that would roll, swinging large branches up and out of the water in menacing gestures. A snaggle of logs approached the Begley swinging bridge. The nurses watched in suspense as a man desperately bolted across mere moments before the unruly raft rammed the bridge, turning it on its side. With a few surges, its planking started snapping, chunks of it splaying downstream. The cables swayed with tension as the rest of the decking was dislodged, but miraculously the cables held.

There was nothing to do but return to the hospital. Just after noon, a call came in that a midwife was needed in a hurry up Beech Fork at the Morton home. Donna and Francis again climbed into the Jeep, hoping their route via the road to Harlan would somehow be passable. They made some progress in that direction, since the road follows the path of the river but at a higher elevation. "The river has now surpassed any high tide I've ever seen before!" Donna exclaimed. They passed a home that had literally turned on its foundation to a cockeyed angle. The place looked vacant but alongside the road they saw sad-looking stacks of dishes, some furniture, and soaked bedding.

Not far beyond that, they were stopped by a gaping washout. Francis was first to get out of the Jeep, wishing in vain for some way around the impasse. Her shoulders slumped with discouragement until she spotted the boy holding a boat, waiting for them. The family had anticipated this and sent him to bring them across. Donna backed the Jeep into the safest place she could find and the women handed over their saddlebags to the boy, and seated themselves in the boat. After a few unsteady circles in the current the boy got the boat aimed at the other side. In the midst of logs and other debris that threatened to capsize them, he managed to navigate safely across, where the father waited in a truck.

Although very shy, the boy admitted that they had started from home at ten that morning to fetch the nurses. It was now past two-thirty in the afternoon. The boy hoisted himself and the nurses' bags into the bed of the truck, and the women squeezed into the cab. The man eased the clutch. "I misdoubt we'll be able to get very fur, but I c'n save you a piece by shanksmares," he said. He drove until the wheels started to spin, and rather than get hopelessly stuck, he shut off the engine and they all took off on foot, crossing a field deep with mud. Donna slipped and tumbled, and the bag with both flashlights slammed to the ground. She knew there would be no electricity in the home, and the thought of no flashlights added to her anxiety. "Next time, pack flashlights in separate bags," she noted to herself.

The constant question in a Frontier nurse's mind was always, "Will I arrive in time to help the woman and her baby?" Donna was beginning to plan for what the nurses called "BBA" – birth before arrival. With the flood delay, and a bit of distance yet to traverse, both nurses wrestled with growing anxiety. There was no way to hurry. The deep mud gripped and clung to their boots, slowing them to an aggravating pace. It was unlikely, but what if the woman needed a Caesarean section? She'd have to be taken to Hyden in these near-impossible conditions – a dreadful thought.[7]

They approached the creek. Early in her FNS career, Donna had learned to use depth markers – taking note of a conspicuous rock or tree root at the place you'd ford a creek, as a way to measure how deep the water was. All her familiar marks were submerged that day. The man couldn't offer much encouragement. The water had risen since he and his boy had crossed earlier, so they grasped each other's wrists and made their way through the powerful current. Donna reached the other side first, and held fast to an emerging root, and pulled the others to safety. They wended along the highest terrain they could find on the final approach to the home, which was situated on bottom land just beyond the creek. That makes for an ideal place for a home – except during a flood.

---

[7] FNS techniques were so successful that by April 1951 there had been only 40 deliveries by Caesarean section in their first 8,596 births. FNS *Quarterly Bulletin*.

The mother had had a sound idea when to send her husband and son for help. Although hard pains were coming on, she reached her arm out in greeting with a warm smile, relieved to see the nurses, no matter their disheveled condition. Her husband had pulled a drop-leaf table near her bed to make some work space for the nurses. It was a spacious home by local standards, and pretty well furnished, but dim in the fading late afternoon light. The family had brought pails of well water into the kitchen, and had filled the kerosene lamps and cleaned their glass chimneys. The water was placed on the step stove to boil.

The nurses removed their muddy boots, and hung their wet outerwear throughout the place to dry. Donna rinsed her hands in some of the water, which looked only slightly cleaner than her hands. She rinsed with Lysol and checked the mother's vitals and dilation. They finished washing up and put on their aprons and caps. Francis laid the saddlebags over a chair, took out and lit the Sterno and set up to sterilize their tools and gloves. While they waited for the water to boil, she laid out all the supplies according to the FNS set-up sheet, which she'd memorized. The important task took her mind off the overfull creek.

"What an uncomfortable feeling, to be in the middle of a delivery and hear the creek whisking by outside," Donna thought. During a moment when she could relax her concentration on the mother, Donna pointed out to the other nurse a water line about knee height, on the inside wall of the room – where the last flood had left its vile mark.

"We can take some comfort that this place has survived awful high water in the past," Donna commented.

The baby arrived after dark, with the help of the battered flashlights. Selecting a newborn's name is a very personal family decision, but Donna couldn't resist whispering to her colleague, "Maybe they'll name him 'Noah' on account of the flood."

The eldest daughter prepared hot soup and huge cat's head biscuits for everyone, by the light of a kerosene lamp. Another child made ready a bed so the nurses could sleep over. Attempting the return journey in the dark would have been folly. Wishing to conserve the drinking water for the mother, the nurses restricted the use of what clean water remained. After a flood unleashes its wicked powers on creatures, land and buildings, it usually insults people by fouling their wells. It was a long and thirsty night for everyone except the healthy newborn, who nursed eagerly.

The next morning the father walked the nurses back to the truck. With good intentions to provide them a drink, he emptied his Prince Albert tobacco, bent the can into a cup, and held it under a shrubby overhang to catch some unsullied water to share. But thirsty as they were, the nurses declined, not comfortable that water from some dripping hillside was free of typhoid or worms.

In her account of the 1947 flood, Mary Breckinridge wrote:

> For weeks after the floods, all through July, it rained
> almost incessantly. When people could get the foul river
> water flushed out of their houses, and their quilts washed
> – then nothing would dry out.

No matter how determined people were in washing their clothing and linens, and scrubbing walls and floors, the fetid smell of mildew permeated their homes. But that was a trifle compared to the livestock, crops, topsoil, lumber, fencing and other property that scattered downstream never to be recovered.

Mrs. Breckinridge concluded her report on the flood, writing, "People suffered more heavily than we had thought credible."

Wendover swinging bridge in the 1947 flood before it washed out — *Reid family photo.*

Hyden during the 1947 flood – *Reid family photo.*

High water rearranges the buildings and swamps out the garden goods downriver of Hyden during 1947 flood – *Reid family photo.*

Stranded mid-river, 1947 flood
— *Reid family photo.*

The people of the flooded counties welcomed the Red Cross aid. Because so much cultivation had been lost during the prime growing season, some assistance came in the form of garden seed and canning jars. The Red Cross had also identified late-season corn and soybean seed that would have a chance of yielding something before the fall frost. Feed for the cows was brought in so the children would continue to have milk. People who before had rebuffed charity, accepted the seed and canning jars, as it gave them a way to work themselves out of the disaster. The FNS organized folks who had not been so affected to haul manure in, to restore the denuded garden patches. The *Thousandsticks News*, in its June 25, 1947 issue, reported that "the people are going about cleaning up and taking it in its course."

When Donna and Francis made their first post-partum visit, the floodwaters had receded and the household was beginning to return to normal. The parents welcomed them, and repeated how thankful they were that the nurses had been able to attend their new baby boy's birth in spite of the trouble that horrible night.

"We was so thankful, we named him after you'uns," the father said.

The nurses looked at each other, their eyebrows lifted.

"Meet Donald Frank Morton," he continued, beaming and holding the newborn out for them.

The nurses were speechless. They knew that parents sometimes named baby girls after midwives.

"This must be a first in FNS history," Donna thought, smiling with pride as she held the infant.

Peace, Pavement, Profits and Poverty

"It's rich country all right,
but you can't eat hardwood, softwood or coal.
And you can't sell the tides."

— Ellery Shields

There was a time before the War when Leslie County families earned less than five hundred dollars a year on average, a sliver of the rest of the nation's income. How did they support themselves and a crop of growing children on one dollar and thirty-seven cents a day?

While most American families slept on store-bought mattresses and Montgomery Ward bed linens, Kentucky highlanders stuffed corn shucks or straw into home-sewn ticking, and laid them over homemade wood frames laced with rope for spring-like support. They would add fragrant sumac or pennyroyal leaves to freshen them. They plucked goose and chicken feathers for downy feather-bed toppers over the crunchy shuck mattress. If their chickens and geese could oblige, feathers went into down pillows as well. Women measured, cut and stitched feed sack prints of dainty florals, plaids, stripes and paislies into quilts, raising the craft to an art form. Their work-roughened hands turned out intricately designed heirlooms with patterns that told stories or bestowed blessings and warmth on their sleeping families.

Most of the nation bought canned goods with colorful labels showing every vegetable and fruit imaginable; mountain people hand-gritted their corn, or soaked it in homemade lye for hominy. Glass jars were hoarded for tomato-canning time, with hopes the preserved crop would last out the year.

City housewives were visited by door-to-door salesmen peddling special-purpose brushes to make their housecleaning easier. Vacuum cleaner salesmen plugged in and demonstrated their miracle machines right in their homes. But Fuller Brush and Hoover vacuum salesmen skipped over the Cumberland Plateau, where homes had no carpet. Nor electricity. Mountain people gathered bark or brown corn from their gardens and tied it to hickory branches for brushes and brooms.

Rural values and rhythms hadn't changed much since settlers had scratched out their "burley patches" and gardens along southeast Kentucky's rivers and creeks a century and a half ago. But that was shifting now. The Civilian Conservation Corps was bringing fine paved roads into the area. There was now a "Three C" road between Hyden and Hazard. You could drive to Harlan, Corbin and London. The method of paying off their babies with installments of guinea hens, honey or potatoes was changing, as mobility enabled people to get paying jobs in the larger towns.

After the Japanese surrender ended World War II, American soldiers came home to the peaceful aftermath. Most found married, domestic life suitable and set off the baby boom. Across America, tidy new suburban houses sprouted like mushrooms after a spring rain. Electricity energized tasks at work and home. Manufacturing, shipping, and consuming demanded combustibles to keep everything in motion, right down to the spin cycle on a new washing machine. The compressor in the modern Frigidaire hummed in the background, keeping after-work beverages cold, while the new electric oven silently heated a casserole and baby bottles warmed on the stovetop. The demand for energy spiked.

Kentucky veterans were returning to a different kind of opportunity than the quiet farm and garden places they'd left. American industry craved more coal to burn, and the Cumberland Plateau sprawled over that deep layer of black gold. New roads meant that coal could be trucked to the railroad. A new platoon of industrialists hired men to work round-the-clock shifts, carving into Kentucky's earth to turn out voltage and heat to make cars, appliances, farm machinery and bridges for a nation whose population was swelling like never before in its history.

"A big workin' mine means royalties fer some land owners, but most o' the money jus' runs right on out o' here once the coal hits the railroad," Ellery explained to Donna. "People ownin' stock in them big minin' companies make money without gettin' dirty. The only thing the fellers workin' the mines take home is coal dust. The comp'ny store gets ever'thing else."

Ellery was close to hitting the bull's-eye of another huge irony. This region, so rich in raw energy, was one of the last in the country to get electricity. The nation's power grid revealed a conspicuous blank in the Cumberland Plateau, with Leslie, Clay and Perry Counties at its heart. Because so few residents could afford the service, electricity didn't reach Hyden until 1948. Leslie County, with a population of fifteen thousand, could boast only one hundred and fifty telephones and a switchboard that operated twelve hours a day. Electric and phone wires were slow to string into the homes farther up the hollows.

While the coal market was robust, mines called for more production. Men answered the call because it meant fatter paychecks. Everyone connected to the mines seemed to be on an endless road to prosperity. Deep-shaft coal mining required a lot of men at the wooden end of a coal shovel. But when mechanized strip mining began replacing manual mining, men were replaced by huge draglines, excavators, loaders and haul trucks bigger than most people's homes. One man on a machine could do the work of a dozen. And they did. The machines ground to a stop just long enough for the man coming on shift to take the controls.

But like zucchini after a perfect summer, when everyone has a good crop, supply overgrows demand. As coal production increased, the industrial appetite shifted from coal to oil. The value of coal dropped. Owners shuttered the mines that had the highest costs: those most distant to the end user, or more pointedly, mines where the labor union had created friction trying to improve safety, working conditions, and pensions.

In 1948, the coal boom in Kentucky went bust. Men showed up at mine entrances day after day, hoping for a sign that there was work for them. Many men left the area for better job opportunities beyond the mountains. When they returned for a weekend or vacation, they shared details of the different lifestyles out there. To some of the home folks, it was all the temptation they needed to move out.

The Frontier nurses updated their records of families that had seen members leave. "It's such rich country with its water and woods," Donna remarked to Ellery. "Isn't there a way these men can stay and support their families like before the War?"

"It's rich country all right, but you can't eat hardwood, softwood or coal. And you can't sell the tides," he said simply. "And folks get mighty tired o' eatin' cushaw by the time they turn their gardens under."

"It's good you have the FNS job," she offered.

"Yeah, but as you know, we're down to two dozen horses. Jeeps are takin' over their place in the stables. The job's a'changin', plain as sundown."

Mrs. Henry Ford had given the FNS its first military-style Jeep. The nurses named it "Jane." It was indeed plain. The athletic little vehicle proved its usefulness – once the nurses learned how to get it to go, stop, and back up. The dogs approved of the vehicle.

"Panda loves the Jeep," said Evelyn. "He rides shotgun with me, watching for squirrels to cross the road!"

Ellery's prediction was coming true. The beloved Tennessee Walkers were giving way to four-wheeled travel. The vehicles, with their protective canvas tops, were preferred on the evolving graded roads, especially in the rain.

But there was no way a Jeep could replace the companionship of a horse.

Horses were still the only practical way the nurses could serve their patients up the narrow creeks, or when the river tide was high. "A lot of our roads are real car-busters, so we'd rather take horses over the rocky places," Donna said. Most of the nurses found sensible reasons to take the horses. But by 1947, the FNS had added a small lineup of surplus war Jeeps from the Willys Motor Company in Toledo. The nurses christened them with endearing names from Charles Dickens novels, like "Mr. Turveydrop." The service station kept track of each Jeep's service records by name, just as Ellery kept track of the animals' shoeing schedules by name.

"Since my dad had the accident with the mule, he hain't been able to work as much, and they've come upon hard times," Ellery explained to Donna. Mr. Shields had been logging with his mule, and when he tried to chain up a felled tree among the brambled limbs, he lost his footing and the startled animal kicked him in the head. "It weren't the mule's fault," Ellery defended. "You'd lash out too if a full-growed man come up right behind you and frashed you."

Donna understood Ellery's affection for the animal. Of course her compassionate friend deeply regretted the accident. His father had been strong and self-reliant, and now the family had to take turns caring for him.

"I'm thinkin' to apply at the deep-shaft mine up Hurricane, as I know it will open back up, and most o' the fellers is gone to get jobs outside," he said. "It pays okay and I c'n still do some o' the blacksmithin' as needed."

"What about your apple orchard, Ellery?" asked Donna.

He paused a long moment, looked at her, and his face brightened into a beautiful smile. "I don't mean to be proud, but I've put a little money down on that piece o' property I been eyin'. I'm makin' payments on time. By and by, I c'n start a'plantin' trees." He had planned this out, but hadn't wanted to be immodest by bringing it up. "Hit's good security for the owner . . . I mean, seller. If I cain't pay it off, he gets back the land and the trees." Ellery looked into Donna's blue eyes. She watched his face soften as he gazed at her hair that the summer sun had lightened to a shade somewhere between sorrel and palomino.

"Why . . . Ellery, I'm *so* pleased for you!" she cried. Unable to contain her joy, she fell into his embrace, and he kissed her. There was no uncertainty in his touch. Donna felt a radiance begin in her heart as she yielded. Even her fingertips tingled. He was gentle but passionate and she was lost in her own ardor as he held her.

Keeping hold of his hands, she leaned back to look him in the eye. "But I worry about anyone working in the mines." She felt a sudden new surge of protectiveness, and squeezed his hands. "We see too many injuries."

There were fewer and fewer well-paying jobs. Cash drifted out of the community like smoke from a smoldering fire, never to return. Rather than leave family tracts they'd lived on for generations, many families signed up for the government's Needy Family Program. Dependence became a weft thread in the weave of society. The commodities program changed the very fabric of some folks' traditional, proud self-reliance.

"People are beginnin' to look in their mailboxes fer income instead o' workin' their woods and gardens," Ellery said. "Now they're linin' up fer gov'mint handouts."

"Sometimes there's things that folks ain't turned to," one woman told Donna. "We had to take a whole sack o' grapefruit. And we didn't know how to use 'em. We boiled 'em, we fried 'em. We tried everything. And we threw 'em over the hill and even the hogses wouldn't eat 'em." [8]

It takes a lot of bread to feed a family of five or six children, and bread was getting harder and harder to win. The only legal birth control method had been a little gizmo patented in 1935 called the "Scientific Prediction Dial." It had introduced the science of fertility timing to women's lives. In 1944, a life-changing, pocket-sized instrument of modernity was making its way into the hollows. The patented "RythMeter" was a more detailed, accurate calculator to determine a woman's ovulation cycle.

Before the scientific dial, women had shared whispered recipes for herbal douches they could prepare in the privacy of their homes to try to prevent pregnancy. If an unwelcome pregnancy occurred, they tried elixirs to induce a miscarriage. Potent blends

[8] – paraphrased from a quote by Grace Reeder, Frontier Nursing Service Oral History Project, 1979.

of the herbs savin and pennyroyal made up the "female prepara-tions" of unknown dosage or risk. Over time, women became less shy about asking FNS nurses for counseling on safe family plan-ning options.

"There have always been what they call 'woods colts' or 'come by chance' children, but most women now believe in contracep-tion within the confines of marriage," Miss Gilbert had lectured. "Our goal is to provide safe and medically-sound guidance."

The FNS referred women through Hyden for the option of tubal ligation, the "tying" – cutting and cauterizing – of the fallo-pian tubes to prevent ova from migrating to the uterus.

One of Miss Gilbert's registered mothers said it this way: "Knowing these things will keep 'em from having babies they don't need.' [9]

"So," Miss Gilbert told the nurses, "know you are sharing valu-able knowledge with our mothers. We want to make them comfort-able asking us about voluntary parenthood."

As the coal boom was collapsing, Harry Truman stood on a stage in Philadelphia accepting the Democratic Presidential nom-ination. With his vice presidential nominee – Kentucky Senator Alben Barkley – at his side, Truman proclaimed:

> "Never in the world were the farmers of any republic or any kingdom or any other country as prosperous as the farmers of the United States . . . Wages and salaries in this country have increased from twenty-nine billion dollars in 1933 to more than one hundred twenty-eight billion in 1947. The total national income has increased from less than forty billion dollars in 1933 to two hundred and three billion in 1947, the greatest in all the history of the world. These benefits have been spread to all the people, because it is the business of the Democratic

---

[9] Quote of Carolyn Gay, FNS Oral History Project, January 1979, Brutus, Kentucky.

Party to see that the people get a fair share of these things."

Senator Barkley had thirty-five years' experience serving Kentucky's people. Donna and others wondered why he didn't gasp in shock at Truman's lofty words that July night in 1948.

The morning after that radio broadcast, neighborhood chatter at the post office was animated.

"There they go jaw-waggin' about the good times while us'uns hain't see'd any more ways to make our livin' by," one man complained.

"Our Senator is gettin' above his raisin' and has fergot all about us," added another.

The candidates touted the late Franklin D. Roosevelt's New Deal, but the prosperity Mr. Truman referred to had settled elsewhere. Many of Senator Barkley's mountain Kentuckians were scrounging up ginseng or beeswax to sell for enough cash to bring a pair of shoes home for their children.

Too Far for Neighboring

*"And let us not be weary in well-doing:
for in due season we shall reap, if we faint not."*

— Paul's letter to the Galatians, 6:9

"If this country were flattened out, we'd be all the way to Pittsburgh by now," Hannah quipped as they dismounted in front of the tiny building that served as the district clinic up Bull Creek.

Clinic day for Donna and Hannah meant getting up and dressed before dawn this April morning. Their route out of Hyden was better suited for horseback, so they'd grained and watered their horses before eating their own breakfast of griddle cakes and game sausage. There were no imminent births, so they prepared their regular nursing bags. Returning to the barn, they gave the horses' backs a few quick brushstrokes before laying on saddle blankets and saddles. They were underway before six o'clock. It would be a couple of hours in the undermountain before the sun topped the spring-green canopy of hardwoods. The season of frost was past and the air promised to be shirt-sleeve pleasant before long. The damp trail smelled of fresh ferns, and the redbud was beginning to bloom. The soulful call of a whip-poor-will harked through the trees, then trailed off.

For Donna, it was one of those days you were filled with the joy of promise. Folks of leisure in their white linens could have their refinements; she was content to be right here, right now, setting off from headquarters with an important job to do. Little did she know that her service in the corps of the Frontier Nursing Service was about to end.

Mrs. Breckinridge sent word with a courier for Evelyn to meet her for tea in the big house next time she was near Wendover. Evelyn was not sure what to expect. She'd been scolded before by Mrs. Breckinridge, and yet her way of talking always seemed to challenge a person to become better.

After greetings, they sat with their tea in the easy chairs in front of the big fireplace. There was no fire, so it offered nothing in the way of diversion. The room was unusually still, except for the tinkle of their cups on the saucers.

"My dear," the senior woman began, her blue eyes boring right into Evelyn's. "I recognize in you a capacity to take risks . . . "

Evelyn understood the absolute need *not* to take risks in nursing tasks. Her mind started spinning, trying to anticipate what the woman meant.

"Not in your nursing, which has been documented as of high standards. No, my dear, your bedside approach is not at issue."

Issue? Was she getting scolded again? wondered Evelyn.

"What you have gained here could be of great value beyond the mountains. You have what I shall call a *willingness to challenge.*" Mrs. Breckinridge paused. "And succeed or fail, I see in you an ability to enter the realm of social service or public policy for a greater good."

Evelyn sat, thinking over her words.

"You are valuable as a Frontier nurse," Mrs. Breckinridge concluded, "but please consider what I've said, and know that you would carry with you unique experience only available in this special place, and excellent recommendations, should your aspirations take you beyond the mountains."

Donna and Hannah unsaddled and tied the horses and before allowing the gathering patients in, checked supplies and swept out rodent nests. Donna conducted a thorough examination of the small structure, looking in likely warm dark places to scare off any copperheads or rattlers that had settled in. Because they could eat vermin up to the size of a squirrel, Donna valued snakes. "But I sure don't want one as a roommate," she always said.

Gathering creekwater for the horse — *Reid family photo.*

Small, non-resident district clinic — *courtesy of FNS.*

The nurses spent the rest of the morning giving tetanus shots, examining odd lumps and bumps, and answering questions. A woman complained of bloody diarrhea and a sore tongue and mouth, indicating a case of pellagra, so Hannah spent extra time with her, explaining the importance of fresh foods. Now that spring had arrived, she was to earnestly look for green onion-like poke, or shoots of collard greens, crow's foot, plantain or dandelions – anything fresh to eat until her garden produce came on. A teenager had an abscess on the outside of his foot where a tender, red streak under his skin was starting up his leg – an early case of blood poisoning. The nurses gave him penicillin and ordered him to lie still with his leg elevated as soon as he got home.

"But how am I to hunt squirrels now that they're a'comin' out o' hibernatin'?" he asked.

"If you ever want to hunt squirrels again, you'll stay off that leg till the redness disappears," Hannah scolded him. Carelessness over blood poisoning, especially in an extremity like a foot, could lead to streptococci infection, or worse, sepsis.

They finished at the little facility, rechecked supplies, jotted the last of the records in the family files then prepared the horses and headed upstream to a routine pre-natal visit. It was time to eat, so they looked for a warm grassy spot off the trail where they could relax a moment with their sandwiches. The only open area was near a family cemetery, which was not unusual. Donna had passed it before, but she never had any reason to stop there. They tied the horses to a pretty beech tree and looked over the stone monuments as they sat eating.

A familiar name caught Donna's eye. There were several stones engraved with it. Shields was Ellery's last name. The women had happened onto his family plot. Donna walked over to a pair of modest stones and read:

Anna Louise Mason   Bonnie Ann Shields
Shields   1939
1918 - 1939

Born into
Giving life gained   Almighty arms
eternity

Ellery lost both his young wife and child during birth. Evidently here was one woman the FNS had let down – one of the statistics on the wrong side of the FNS success story. A wave of anger gripped Donna. They had let Ellery down, too.

"You're awfully quiet, Donna," Hannah commented as they rode up the trail. "Did you pick up one of those 'hants' at the cemetery?"

"You could put it that way, I guess," she allowed, still moved by what she'd seen. They arrived at the pre-natal, and as Hannah was checking Thelma, Donna noticed a wooden goods-box that had handmade rockers added for a cradle. There was a beautiful baby quilt folded neatly in it.

"I'm so pleased to see that you've made such a nice place for the baby," the nurse said to Thelma. This couple had kept their previous baby in bed with them for convenience while it was still nursing. But tragically, neither parent awoke in the night as the baby gasped its last breath from suffocation beneath the heavy covers.

"Yes. Kress and I lost a lot of sleep over that. The idee o' losin' a least one like that has left a fear in us to this day." The three women were silent a moment as the awful recollection passed.

Thelma then told the nurses of another woman in need – a very imminent birth. "She's a bit too far for neighboring . . . two, maybe three miles yon," which was farther out of their way.

"I'd be much pleased if you made the time to check in on her. Maybe it can give her new one a' comin' a better chance, gettin' some care from you'uns," Thelma said. She handed them two hard boiled brown eggs and began wrapping in newspaper a large square of cornbread she'd split and filled with molasses. "Yes, I'd be much pleased," she repeated as she thrust the package at them.

The mother Thelma referred to was a "non-registered," having chosen not to notify the closest nursing center of her pregnancy. She had had none of the prenatal care that registered women received from the Frontier nurses. Maybe it was the money. More likely, this remote family hung to old notions that stretched back to a time before the FNS was generally accepted and trusted. Whatever the reason, or her status with the Service, it did not stop the two traveling nurses from hurrying to her side, now that she needed help.

They were grateful for the dry spring day, although by now the sun had already passed below the high, wooded horizon.

They found the home. It had no glass for the windows, only wooden shutters on hinges. The shanty sagged on decrepit footings, barely above the ground.

"Looks like our only defense against snakes will be our boots," Hannah said. In the shadows, Donna thought it seemed a gloomy place, with some throw-aways about the clearing. But all that mattered was what they found inside. It was poorly furnished and there were flies by the hundred.

Janie had already commenced labor and was in great discomfort. Her husband came in, evidently from working their plantings. The nurses improvised what they needed, then sent their older boy back to the hospital – a ten-mile round trip – with a flashlight and a list of more complete delivery supplies. More light was needed, so the man lit kerosene lamps and an old miner's carbide lamp, which gave off a strong chemical smell. It was going to be a long night. Chinks in the wood stove glowed orange as kettles of water were boiled. Blessedly, the wood shutters could be propped open to the night air to freshen the close room.

The nurses refused the food that the man offered, knowing this family no doubt needed everything they had in their larder, especially with the addition of a new baby. Nor were they comfortable with the sanitary conditions. There was no outhouse. FNS nurses always carried a couple of candy bars for quick energy, but the two women reserved those, and unwrapped and ate what Thelma had packed for them.

The birth progressed slowly because the baby was presenting backwards. This would have caused serious complications for an untrained attendant, but Donna patiently and gently got the baby turned. With a few more hard pushes by the mother, the birth proceeded safely. By then, it was getting light in the east, and they were all exhausted except the newborn. The father had seen to plenty of boiling water and the nurses bathed the baby and mother. After fifteen hours on this case, Donna and Hannah were able to leave them in satisfactory condition.

Fatigued but duty-bound, the pair conducted visits on the way back to Hyden. They made three sick calls, and checked in on a post-partum mother and her new baby.

At long last they arrived back at Hyden, nearly drained, at 10:30 in the morning. The women had spent twenty-eight hours on duty or traveling, with only what they could carry in their saddlebags for comfort and sustenance, and without complaints. A glass of fresh water, hot wash water, a meal, and a bed was their most comforting compensation.

When Donna settled into her dorm room for an hour's rest, she reflected on the long day's accomplishments. She thought of Janie giving birth in that crude home, and the mother's reluctance at first to consider the nurse's help. Donna and Hannah had earned far more than a day's pay. They had earned someone's trust. It was a small victory – just one more family among many – but Donna knew that their care had influenced the health and future of that little family up the hollow all by themselves.

Donna was given the entire next day off. She had no reason to think there was more of a purpose than some well-deserved leisure. Fully rested, she got up early to enjoy another Kentucky spring day and to catch up on some nursing periodicals.

She couldn't place a date on when it happened, but Kentucky mountain life had become as much a part of her as the fragrance of conifers is part of the forest. Although not kin, Donna knew she had been completely accepted and valued for her role in the well-being of these families. She didn't dwell on it, but the notion gave her a satisfied feeling.

Her thoughts returned to Ellery and his loss. He "had no family as of this time," like he'd said that day in the garden.

The smell of biscuits and coffee brought her back to the present and she finished dressing for breakfast.

Mrs. Breckinridge joined her after the meal. After pouring each of them a cup of coffee, she looked squarely at Donna and told her they'd received some news from Donna's people in Michigan. Her widowed aunt had had a serious accident and was in the hospital. She would be laid up a long while. Placing her hand on Donna's arm, Mrs. Breckinridge looked at her with deep empathy.

In the silence that followed, a Kentucky warbler burbled a good morning lilt.

Donna felt a twinge deep in her heart. Did this mean she would have to leave her position with the FNS? Leave Ellery? She had never really thought out an ending to her life of serving people in Kentucky. What about Ellery's orchard?

Donna knew Myra's neighbors would do what they could until she arrived, but they all had their own demands. Returning to care for Myra and keep the family farm going was the way she could finally return the care and devotion Myra had given Donna and her sisters when their mother died. She always knew circumstances at home might someday take her away from Kentucky, but her heart pounded in curt disagreement with the rational decision she knew she had to make. Leaving this place and the fulfillment she'd discovered here would be like trying to take the echo out of the canyon.

Mrs. Breckinridge said she understood Donna's strong sense of duty to her family and was prepared to accept that she would – for a time – be losing "an *excellent* nurse-midwife who'd stepped up to all challenges with never a complaining word." There would always be a place for her in the FNS, the founder said.

The praise made Donna feel even more reluctant to leave the camaraderie and her meaningful Frontier Nursing duties. But she took a deep breath and resolved to face this new bend in her path. "If one has to leave their duty, it's best to leave with laurels," she decided. Knowing she could hand off her patients to caring and able colleagues gave her comfort. It was then Donna could accept the situation with her customary can-do spirit; a spirit that she had brought with her to the Frontier Nursing Service, and that had been strengthened by caring for the mountain folks under some extreme circumstances.

She found Hannah, and shared her news. She tried to cover her heartache. "Be sure to pass along my best wishes to Janie on your next post-partum visit," Donna said in the brightest voice she could manage.

Evelyn had heard the news and made her way to Hyden so she could sympathize and be with her friend. They'd shared so many extraordinary times. It was thanks to Evelyn that Donna had become a Frontier nurse, and she would be ever grateful for that.

"Oh Donna, I hate to see you go after all we've been through!" Evelyn gushed. "We know you'll always have a place to fill here!"

"I hate to go, too, but it must be . . . for a time. Lucky for you, you can stay as long as you like!"

"Well-l-l . . . " Evelyn began, "Mrs. Breckinridge met with me privately last week. She was firm, and told me some things that will change my future, too."

Donna looked at her, astonished. "What do you mean?"

"I'm going beyond the mountains to do some serious fundraising, and then maybe work into a position with the state. I'm *so* passionate about our work and Mrs. Breckinridge wants me to use my connections . . . " Evelyn trailed off. "But Donna, right now, let's get everyone together for a party before you have to go! We want to give you a proper send-off! It'll help lift our spirits!"

"Please, no. Let's not interrupt the work. I really must get ready to leave right away. Myra needs me most now."

"Oh Donna, these last half-dozen years . . . I couldn't think of *anything* better!"

Donna couldn't express herself any better, either. "Me too," were the only words she could muster, and the two young women embraced. Donna wiped her eyes and nose with the only thing she had at the moment, the back of her hand.

She went to her room, closed her door and allowed her thoughts to venture beyond the emergency in Michigan. She especially wanted her dad to meet Ellery, and for Ellery to meet the rest of her family in their surroundings. Donna began packing, and Ardice stopped by to say she'd take her to the next train. "You'll be missed *greatly*, Donna," Ardice said, "and I'm speaking for *everyone!*"

Always self-conscious when praised, Donna continued packing. "I'll miss you all, too," she said humbly, overwhelmed by her own emotions.

She went outside to say good-bye to Jefferson.

"I'll always be grateful for you getting me where I was needed, Jeff," she said, stroking his long neck. "That time the cinch strap

broke, and you stopped and waited there beside the creek until
I realized the trouble . . . I could have ended up with my head
against the rocks . . . "

There was no more time to reminisce about the adventures
they'd shared.

"They'll take good care of you, Bucky," she said, more to soothe
her own feeling of loss. "You've proven yourself, time and again."
She choked up as she petted the loyal little dog. Ardice had promised Donna that another nurse would adopt him so he could stay
with the Service.

Then she found Ellery. She gave him the news. In his typical way,
only his eyes showed emotion at first, but then his body slumped
with disappointment. His gaze settled on hers. They stood in silence for a long moment. He reached for her hands and held them.
Donna promised she would be back. She started speaking without
thinking but she went on anyway, saying, "just as soon as my situation
allows for me to return."

"I would be much, much pleased, only after you've taken care
of family needs, Donna."

After an awkward silence, he continued.

"Y'know, I didn't think I'd ever ag'in know a woman as fine as .
. . as my lost wife. She and her mother drove t' Manchester fer suitable baby things, and after that car hit 'em broadside, she never
really recovered. And the nurses here did ever'thing they could
when it come time fer the baby, but . . . "

The two of them closed in together in a long embrace, feeling
each other's heartbeats. They released, and Donna eventually found
words, trying to buoy the weight of the moment. "Ellery, I didn't
come to Kentucky thinking I'd find such a fine man, either . . . "

Maybe she could return in time to help him begin planting
those apple trees, she said, but her voice broke off. His eyes brightened, and a smile spread across his face that started from deep
inside. Donna would long remember that goodbye kiss and the way
he looked at her.

At the Hazard station, she hefted her bag onto the vestibule. She felt as if her heart was loaded with sand as she stepped up and boarded the northbound train.

"Quick goodbyes are best," she thought. "Less lingering over leaving."

She stared out the window, and blinking through her tears, she watched the familiar mountains slowly turn to rolling greens of open space. She had dedicated her hands and her soul to life here. She couldn't imagine calling any other place "home" and she pictured Ellery solidly in that home. She imagined his strong but gentle arms holding her again. Would he be willing to come north and visit during her time there?

She reflected on the privilege of bringing healthy babies into the world safely. Donna's mind was crowded with memories: the mother's eased mind when an antibiotic conquered her baby's high fever; the little boy's delight when she told him he could go outdoors again; the safe delivery of the Bartell twins; and Rufus Feltner's nice letter to Mrs. Breckinridge thanking Miss Carroll and Miss Lenschow for their kindness. Donna remembered that frosty starlit morning in February and leaving out of the center at two-thirty to deliver their baby. In her mind she saw the gratitude and relief in the eyes of all "her" mothers and fathers.

Donna took a deep breath. She knew that when she greeted her Aunt Myra, she'd see that same grateful relief.

She turned her love and passion toward her current task – to serve her family in Michigan.

That autumn, she received a letter addressed in handwriting she did not recognize. She spotted the Wendover postmark, and immediately opened it.

It read:

> *Dear Miss Donna,*
> *I knowed you would greatly care to learn that we lost*
> *our dear Ellery in a slide fall at the mine. The good news*

is he didn't suffer. They think he was gone before he hit the ground.

It was signed "Sincerely," by his mother, Maybella Shields.

Donna sat in stunned silence. The weight in her chest was nearly unbearable. She finally caught her breath. "He never got to see his apple trees in bloom," she said aloud, clutching the letter with a shaking hand.

There was little time to grieve. Her skills were needed here and now.

She never found another man who made her feel like Ellery had. Instead, she poured her love into nursing and into tending the half-dozen apple trees she'd planted following that devastating letter from Kentucky.

Donna sensed the kind horseshoer's presence every spring when her apple trees blossomed. And in the fall, each time she picked a ripe apple, it was like reaching up and touching his hand.

Conclusion

"I have fooled them before."

– Doris Reid

<hr>

*H*aving shared a fictionalized version of part of my Aunt Doris's abundant life, I'd like to share the real-life story of her death. Doris approached it with the same steady, stalwart, take-charge attitude with which she always answered the call to serve, regardless of time, distance or travail.

Following her work with the Frontier Nursing Service, which had developed into a supervisory position at the Hyden Hospital, Doris returned to Michigan. She became Cheboygan County's public health nurse, then became nursing supervisor for a four-county area for twenty-two more years. After officially retiring, she continued serving on the Health Advisory Board, giving more than sixty years of her life to public health. Among her many awards was Honorary Fellow of the American College of Nurse-Midwives, and Michigan's most "Be-Involved Nurse." She was so well loved and respected in the counties she served that when a new clinic was constructed in 1992 in the town of Cheboygan, it was named the Doris E. Reid Center.

There wasn't much of a line between on- and off-duty for Doris, and the community benefitted from her competency and caring heart until the end.

She had witnessed birth, illness, injury, healing, sudden death, terminal illness, and slow death. Her twin sister Dorothy had languished and eventually succumbed at age 77 to Amyotrophic Lateral Sclerosis, "Lou Gehrig's" disease. Doris had held many hands along the way, from the labored arrivals of new "least ones" to standing vigil over the last breath of a dying patient, gently ushering death up the aisle to embrace the departed.

I remember a family dinner one summer at the old home place they called Shady Nook on Michigan State Road 68. Doris loved to share her fresh catch or wild game with family, neighbors and friends. Over a checkered oilcloth, we ate fried walleye, home-grown corn on the cob, and sliced cucumbers and tomatoes that just minutes ago had rested in the warm earth not twenty yards from the table. Someone paused long enough to ask Doris if she was expecting any success deer hunting this coming fall, and she quipped, "Well, I have fooled them before."

Suffering her own health complications including a groin artery blockage that was hindering circulation in both her heart and leg, a defective heart valve, and advancing cancer, Doris – at age eight-seven – fully understood the prognosis and what awaited her. Once her capacity to serve others was gone, her reason for living faded. She saw no need to push the final event into the future.

Thinking over her options, she asked her doctor for a frank answer. He knew she expected and deserved nothing less.

"Once taken off oxygen," he said, "you could linger six minutes, six hours or six days."

Her notion not to become someone else's burden was compelling enough for her to select a time: Three o'clock the next Saturday.

In the context of today's passionate debate about end-of-life choices, Doris was a generation ahead of her time. She chose to die with dignity at this time and place. She made the decision to withdraw from the oxygen machine because, she told her caregivers, "That's not a decision I felt I should leave for my family to have to make."

Doris made a list, and all the people she loved were called. If they wanted to see her, they needed to drop by the Petoskey hospital before three o'clock that Saturday in January. With a firm grip and an ageless smile, she greeted each of the many visitors who appeared over the next days.

One of them, a loving second-cousin, trying to find the appropriate words in taking his final leave, told Doris to "take care, and who knows, maybe this fall will find you back hunting deer again." She responded, "I have fooled them before."

The room cleared out a bit before three o'clock on Saturday, January 21, 2001, and as requested, Doris was prepared for the cessation of the life-giving oxygen. She slipped away peacefully six hours later, at nine o'clock that evening.

Afterword

"When your heart speaks, I hear it."
— Julie Marfell, PhD, Frontier School of
Midwifery Chair, to the 58th graduating class
— May 2009

Today in Mary Breckinridge's bedroom, upstairs in the "big house" hangs a framed photo of her standing with a pretty girl in a dress. The girl is about eight years old with shiny bangs and beautiful long hair, and stands nearly as tall as Mrs. Breckinridge. She is Marlene Wooten, the Frontier Nursing Service's ten-thousandth baby, born in 1958.

The big house now operates as a bed and breakfast. It is on the National Historic Register, but it's as homey and embracing as Grandmother's, right down to the faint smell of bacon, castile soap, and the creak of the oak floor. Among the authentic furnishings is a cane-bottom sewing rocker, created by Sherman Wooten. It's a sibling to the chair he presented to the U. S. President, which is now displayed in the Smithsonian. It's easy to imagine a coterie of nurses seated in front of the many bookcases, enjoying tea and conversation. The spirit of the place is nurtured by the housekeeping staff, who carry on the tradition of warmth and abundance. I've never seen bigger biscuits.

While researching this book I enjoyed the privilege of staying in Mary Breckinridge's bedroom, just a pebble-toss above the Middle Fork of the Kentucky River. The stately beech tree – now over two hundred years old – towers outside one window, the frequent soft May rain splashing on its seasonal foliage. Surrounded by the peace that only chinked logs offer a room, I could easily feel how a spirit could be refreshed within the place. With its filtered light coming through the trees, the room was her refuge after a day of ordeals administering to her "wide neighborhoods."[10]

---

[10] *Wide Neighborhoods* is the title of Mrs. Breckinridge's autobiography, published in 1952.

Night brought a slower tempo and I could hear the Middle Fork in the deepening silence. I awoke to the same birdsong Mrs. Breckinridge enjoyed so much, and I padded across the same varnished floorboards to select the day's clothing from the same modest closet. I took for granted that I could snap the light on; she lived in the home twenty-three years before an electric power line brought that convenience to her door.

In 1965 Mrs. Breckinridge died in this room, at the age of eighty-four. But her vision, intensity and dedication to rural, medically-underserved people is as alive today as the persistent Middle Fork that courses below Wendover, thanks to those who carry on her mission.

I was especially fortunate that my first visit coincided with the graduation celebration of the Frontier School of Midwifery "Class of Fifty-Eight"– the fifty-eighth class of clinic-bound nurses. Beginning with the first two graduates in 1939, the tradition continues that the eve before the nurses depart they share a meal in the big house. Twenty-nine graduates plus Dr. Marfell and other faculty gathered in the dining room. Cane-bottom chairs magically appeared as the guest count went up.

They scooped me into their circle, and we joined arms for the traditional singing of "Amazing Grace." With wet eyes, we then sat down elbow-to-elbow at long tables set with Churchill Chelsea blue willow English china. The nurses had spent that afternoon practicing suturing on real pig's feet, and as we passed enormous bowls of steaming food around the table they began sharing graphic details of their day. They clipped the conversation when one young woman cast them a sideward glance in kindly deference to me.

After salad, fried chicken, mashed potatoes, green beans, fresh baked rolls, coffee and apple cake topped with ice cream, we crowded into the sitting room for the seventy-year-old pledging ritual. With William F. Draper's oil portrait of Mrs. Breckinridge gazing at us from above the mantel, each nurse pledged what she would do "with these hands." I was so moved by their sincerity and dedication I could not speak.

A few days later, I reluctantly checked out of the lovely haven. The Middle Fork was smeary and urgent-looking. It was easy to see that the river could assert itself among the big rocks and trees lining its banks.

I understood Aunt Doris's regret at leaving. The mountains embrace you and the water nourishes you, even if it gets angry at times. The people are part of the place, just as a cedar tree belongs along a creek, sheltering the undergrowth. Before I left the area, I searched out a cemetery to locate some headstones. The kind man on the backhoe saw me and stopped his work. When he heard what I was looking for, he pointed me in the right direction. "The Frontier Nursing Service sure does a lot for the people around here," he said. I heard similar sentiments from other Leslie Countians while I was among them.

"They sure made life better in this part of the country . . ."

"Mrs. Breckinridge started something very important . . ."

The FNS kept accurate statistics and continually evaluated its work. In 1932 the Metropolitan Life Insurance Company tabulated the Service's first thousand births, and their official report concluded:

> *The study shows conclusively that the type of service rendered by the Frontier Nurses safeguards the life of mother and babe. If such service were available to the women of the country generally, there would be a saving of ten thousand mothers' lives per year in the United States, there would be thirty thousand less stillbirths and thirty thousand more children alive at the end of the first month of life.*

The FNS, undaunted by isolation, drought, fire, flood, the Depression and world war, continues its work in Kentucky. It has grown and refined, bringing up-to-date care to its people without interruption. The need for rural health care in the region has not gone away. Injuries, accidents, illness and of course births continue. I learned from one of the staff that her uncles were among the thirty-eight killed in the 1970 Finley mine blast, five miles out of Hyden.

In 1975, the new critical-access Mary Breckinridge Hospital opened at the foot of Thousandsticks Mountain in Hyden. As of this writing, the FNS operates five rural healthcare centers and a home-health agency. The Frontier School of Midwifery and Family Nursing is the oldest continuously operating midwifery school in the nation. In 2008 the school added the Doctor of Nursing Practice Program which augments its three graduate nursing tracks. It now operates under the title Frontier Nursing University. The original Hyden oak barn was converted to a classroom, and has been outfitted with internet technology for multi-media instruction. Mardi Cottage serves as a suite of clinical practice rooms, where the midwives practice births on anatomically complete educational models.

Mrs. Breckinridge would be pleased to see that her goal, "to imbue young physicians with our love of the rural areas and their people, so that some of them will be willing to settle in country districts even at a financial sacrifice," is a core value of the curriculum.

Graduates leap borders and waters to serve around the world. The FNS embraced the idea of "wide neighborhoods," fulfilling Mrs. Breckinridge's beginning assertion that "if it can be done here, it can be done anywhere."

The school is outgrowing its current facilities and has drawn plans for a new building on the Hyden property. For information on the current status of the Frontier Nursing Service and how you can help them achieve this goal, go to: http://www.frontier.edu

Acknowledgements

"They say once you've drunk out of the Middle Fork of the Kentucky, you will always want to return."

— Doris Reid, *Saddlebags Full of Memories*

T hroughout the writing of this book, I often wished to slip away from the demands of my present life and return to the deep woods, tumbling waters, and fine people I met in the heart of Kentucky's Cumberland Plateau. I'd taken my drink from the Middle Fork and I, too, wanted to return. In spirit, I did return over and over – from the confines of my home. Soft dialogue would occur to me, and regardless of the time of day or night, it was time to try to capture the rich sorghum timbre of their speech. Throughout it all I was "good pleased."

I wish to thank the fine Kentucky folks for treating this outsider so patiently and sharing their beloved hills and hollows, answers, insights, and lives so graciously with me. I live among mountains, and their mountains are as beautiful as any I've seen.

I wish to thank my parents for seeing to it that I knew Aunt Doris and her family. My mother, Margaret Ritchie Howard, was eight years old when her widowed mother married Doris's father, Frank Reid. Frank and his four children became Mother's stepfamily. Although my parents moved out west during World War II, they had the wisdom to return with their children to Michigan many times while we were growing up. Summer trips always included time at Burt Lake with Doris and her family. We enjoyed the legendary Burt Lake Community Club Corn Roast. During those days wrapped in country tradition, I learned to appreciate Doris's roots, her dedication, and her ways.

I am grateful to my father, Sherman Howard, who, along with my mother, gave me my head so I could pursue my own passions. I was fortunate to own half-breed Tennessee Walkers for much of my young life. I spent a considerable amount of time with them, to the point of misshaping my formative legs. My schoolmates teased me about my bowlegs and knock knees. I can easily conjure up the smell, sounds and thrill of horsemanship, the warmth of a horse's withers on a cold or rainy day, and the camaraderie of a seasoned trail horse. I also recognize the deep fatigue from a long day in the saddle. From the balls of your feet to the base of your neck, you want a hot soak as soon as the tack is put away. Rarely could Doris look forward to that luxury.

I want to thank my four children for enriching my life as a mother, and for becoming independent so I could turn my attention to writing. May each of you find something that yields the pleasure I've found writing this book.

Sincere appreciation goes to: Louella Elya Mosciski, Doris's niece, for her support and for providing a box full of Doris's Frontier Nursing Service mementoes; and Honorable Alton T. Davis, Lansing, Michigan, Doris's second cousin who shared the precious memory of his final visit with her.

A huge measure of gratitude goes to my mentor and lay editor, Mary Barmeyer O'Brien, author of a collection of excellent books on Western pioneers for Globe Pequot Press. Mary encouraged me from the conception of this book, and has guided me along the way. I also want to thank Maggie Plummer, author of "Spirited Away – A Novel of the Stolen Irish" for her editing expertise and enthusiasm; Paul Fugleberg, editor emeritus of the Flathead Courier and Ronan Pioneer, whose journalistic accomplishments are too numerous to mention here. For seventeen years, I was enriched by working alongside him during hectic deadline days at our weekly newspapers. Paul taught me to respect deadlines and pace myself for the long haul, much like a good walking horse does.

In addition, thanks go to

- Frontier Nursing Service personnel: especially Michael Claussen in the Development office, and his excellent staff at the Big House in Wendover; AnnDraia Bales; Barb Gibson, Assistant to FNS CEO;
- Julie Marfell, PhD., Frontier School of Midwifery Chair, Dept. of Family Nursing / Course Coordinator, for her

inspiration and for allowing me to observe the traditional graduation ceremony of the school's fifty-eighth graduating class;

- Kentucky State Library staff member Doug Boyd and Jason Flahardy, for providing access and digital versions of the nearly two hundred cubic feet of archival material and the amazing Frontier Nursing Service Oral History Project;
- Polson, Montana City Library staff members for hauling the interlibrary loan books back and forth from the post office; their help and good cheer has been of great value to my research;
- Mac Swan, for his proofreading assistance and special appreciation, as his mother was from nearby Floyd County, Kentucky;
- Hyden, Kentucky Public Library staff; Hazard, Kentucky Public Library staff; The *Hazard Herald* newspaper staff; *Hyden News,* and *Thousandsticks News* staff;
- U.S. Forest Service Red Bird District Office
- and the many printed and electronic resources relating to the Frontier Nursing Service.

I will not attempt to include all the incredible people who were part of the experiences Doris had, but one example deserves special mention: the tireless surgeon, Dr. R. L. Collins of Hyden, who is among the scores of heroes chronicled in Mrs. Breckinridge's 1952 autobiography, *Wide Neighborhoods.* If I have piqued your curiosity I heartily encourage you to read it.

For Further Reading:
Wide Neighborhoods, Mary Breckinridge. University Press of Kentucky, 1952; 1981;
Clever Country, Kentucky Mountain Trails, Caroline Gardner. Fleming H. Revell Co., 1931;
Mary on Horseback, Rosemary Wells. Puffin Books, 1998;
Babies in her Saddlebags, Joyce Hopp. Pacific Press Publishing, 1986;
The Frontier Nursing Service, Marie Bartlett; McFarland and Co., 2008;

A Social History of the Frontier Nursing Service, Nancy Damman. Social Change Press, 1982;

Full Speed Ahead - The Life and Legacy of Kate Ireland, David Treadwell, 2009;

Where Else But Here, Lucille Knechtly. Pippa Valley Printing, Pippa Passes, KY, 1989;

Trails Into Cutshin Country, A History of the Pioneers of Leslie County, Sadie Stidham, 1978;

Nurses on Horseback, Ernest Poole. The Macmillan company, 1932;

Night Comes to the Cumberlands, Harry M. Caudill. Jesse Stuart Foundation, 2001, Originally published by Little, Brown Co., 1963;

A Darkness at Dawn, Harry M. Caudill. Kentucky Bicentennial Bookshelf, 1976;

Yesterday's People, Jack Weller. University Press of Kentucky, 1965;

This Happened in the Hills of Kentucky, John Vogel. Zondervan Publishing House, 1952;

Pioneer Doctor, Mari Graña. Two Dot, Globe Pequot Press, 2005;

More Than Petticoats, Gayle C. Shirley. Two Dot, Globe Pequot Press, 1995;

The Doctor Wore Petticoats, Chris Enss, Two Dot, Globe Pequot Press, 2006;

Far Appalachia, Noah Adams. Dell Publishing, Random House, 2001.

C. Margo Mowbray writes from her home in rural western Montana. Her newspaper career began at age twenty, with proofreading obituaries and legal notices in one of Montana's oldest weeklies. For nearly three decades, she continued in a fulfilling career of printing, and publishing award-winning weekly newspapers. Mowbray serves on her local hospital board and has served in the Montana Senate. She is the mother of four grown children. This is her first novel.

Made in the USA
San Bernardino, CA
18 October 2013